The Other Ones

The Other Ones

Jean Thesman

VIKING

VIKING
Published by the Penguin Group
Penguin Putnam Books for Young Readers, 345 Hudson Street, New York,
New York 10014, U.S.A.
Penguin Books Ltd, 27 Wrights Lane, London W8 5TZ, England
Penguin Books Australia Ltd, Ringwood, Victoria, Australia
Penguin Books Canada Ltd, 10 Alcorn Avenue, Toronto, Ontario, Canada M4V 3B2
Penguin Books (N.Z.) Ltd, 182–190 Wairau Road, Auckland 10, New Zealand

Penguin Books Ltd, Registered Offices: Harmondsworth, Middlesex, England

First published by Viking, a member of Penguin Putnam
Books for Young Readers, 1999

3   5   7   9   10   8   6   4

LIBRARY OF CONGRESS CATALOGING–IN–PUBLICATION DATA
The other ones / Jean Thesman.
p.   cm.
Summary : High school sophomore Bridget Raynes has to decide whether or
not to accept her powers of witchcraft, or abandon them and try to fit in as an
ordinary teenager.
ISBN 0-670-88594-0
[1. Witchcraft—Fiction.   2. Friendship—Fiction.   3. Bullies—Fiction.
4. Aunts—Fiction.   5. High schools—Fiction.   6. Schools—Fiction.]   I. Title.
PZ7.T3525Ot   1999   [Fic—dc21   98-45711   CIP   AC

Printed in the U.S.A.

Set in Bembo

BOOKS BY JEAN THESMAN

The Other Ones
The Moonstones
The Tree of Bells
The Storyteller's Daughter
The Ornament Tree
Summerspell
Cattail Moon
Nothing Grows Here
Molly Donnelly
When the Road Ends
The Rain Catchers
Appointment with a Stranger
Rachel Chance
The Last April Dancers

This is for Sharyn November and her friend who wears purple velvet shoes. They understand the importance of a proper tea.

ᔕᕕᐣ

chapter one

I was the first one who saw her. I didn't hear the door to the English class open, and she stood so still that she didn't even seem to be breathing. I caught my breath, too, and it was as if I had sudden knowledge of a strange place I'd never imagined. I gripped my hands together so hard that they hurt.

It was eight-forty in first period, and Woody McCready was still reading the morning bulletin aloud. He was late finishing it because he'd argued with Mrs. Munson before he began, and now she'd make sure the whole class paid. Why did she ask him to read aloud so often? He hated it, and he did such a terrible job that he embarrassed himself.

Mrs. Munson watched me, not Woody. Her eyes were

narrow and speculative, and she never seemed to blink. She tapped her big teeth with her pencil.

The stranger took one step inside the room, and a quick ripple of awareness spread over everyone in the class except Woody. He struggled on and stumbled over the word *assembly.*

"*Assemaly,*" he said. "No, *assby.*"

No one dared laugh. Not yet, at least.

"*Ass!*" Woody finished triumphantly, and he looked around to see if everyone appreciated his switch from stupidity to colossal wit. He snorted laughter, wiped his nose on the back of his hand, and then saw that he'd lost his audience. Everyone had turned to stare at the stranger.

Immediately I knew that most of the other girls wouldn't like her, and I was already sorry for her. For one thing, starting school after the semester began was a very bad move. I remembered that from my own experience in fourth grade. The girls had already divided into competing cliques, and they had more fun excluding people than including them. Mitzie Coburn and I were always excluded, Mitzie because she was overweight and I because . . . I didn't really know why. Yes, I did. From the beginning, they sensed something about me, no matter how hard I tried to be like everybody else.

The biggest reason the new girl was making instant enemies was the way she looked. She was different in every possible way, but she held her head up as if she knew it and didn't care. She wore a long chevron-patterned brown skirt and a thin ivory-colored shirt instead of the jeans and shorts, tees and sweatshirts that all the rest of us wore. The leather sandals on her bare tan feet looked new. Her long, layered hair was precisely streaked brown and blond and looked as if her hairdresser was a computer instead of a human. It was . . . strange. Her round dark eyes seemed calm enough, facing a class of unsmiling strangers, and I wondered if she was studying us.

She carried a handful of registration papers and a neat brown leather pocketbook. Why was she transferring to Bayhead High now, during the last week of September? I felt around the edges of her mind, looking for an answer, but she closed me out the instant she sensed my question.

Okay. She caught on to me sooner than most.

Woody McCready whispered something to a boy sitting in the front row, and both of them laughed. Then he turned to stare insolently at the newcomer in the doorway. I was sure he wanted to seem important and intimidating. Instead, he only looked mean, with dirt-colored eyes and greasy, dark hair. He and his friends always dressed in black, like TV gang members, but nobody dared laugh. Woody could hit hard. Very hard.

I hated him so much that when I looked at him, my hands automatically turned into fists.

The new girl studied Woody calmly, then looked toward the windows, totally dismissing him.

Oh ho, Woody, I thought. This will be fun. Is she someone you can't bully? But you be careful, new girl. You be really careful. Woody is full of ugly surprises.

I decided at that moment that I wanted to be the new girl's friend.

"Are you coming in, stupid?" Woody asked her. He laughed, as if he'd been clever.

"Come up to the desk," Mrs. Munson told the girl. "Woody, finish the bulletin and then take your seat."

I felt the entire class hold its breath as the new girl walked toward Mrs. Munson's desk. Jennifer Budd, a fake blond with eyes like bright blue marbles, our apprentice beauty contestant and especially unloved by Mitzie and me, whispered furiously to the girl next to her but never stopped gawking at the stranger. Jennifer's jealousy poured out into the room like a sour odor, and the other girls caught the scent. The boys reacted to the girls' animosity with nervous excitement. They muttered and laughed hoarsely, nudging each other.

What a beginning, I thought, pitying the new girl. Wherever she came from must be better than this.

Mrs. Munson glanced through the girl's papers, then said, "People, this is Althea Peale. Althea, sit next to Bridget Raynes. Back there! See? She's the girl in the red shirt!"

It didn't take much to infuriate Mrs. Munson. A split-second's hesitation would do it.

Althea walked to the empty chair beside me, without flinching when the girls snickered and the boys openly laughed at her as she passed. It was her clothes, her attitude, and her strange hair. And her newness. There was no room for her among these kids.

I slid down in my chair and looked out the window at the pale blue sky and the gold and brown trees. I really hated that class, and I'd always liked English before.

Althea's skirt rustled softly when she sat down. She folded her hands and stared straight ahead. A student aide came in then, carrying a thick brown envelope, and Mrs. Munson told us that our school photo I.D.s were ready. When she passed them out, most of the kids made disparaging remarks, even as they showed their photos around, waiting for compliments. Mitzie and I tucked ours into our wallets without comment. Mitzie had glossy dark hair and perfect skin, but she weighed too much. I had light brown hair and my skin was good enough, but I stammered and I was clumsy. I could trip over a dog hair.

In the few minutes left in first period, Mrs. Munson plunged into our class work. When she talked about sentence structure, she sounded as if she might explode into violence any second. If she hated teaching English so much, why did she do it? Why didn't she teach science or math? Or better yet, why wasn't she a prison guard? Or a burglar? I'd heard she didn't have children. I hoped she didn't even have a pet, but I didn't search her mind for answers. She was so mean I didn't want to know what went on inside her thick skull.

I was sure she'd call on me to read my list of adjectives describing weather, and she did. I'd written "dank" at the end of my list, and Woody started off the laughter when he heard it.

"Dank," he whined through his nose. "Daaank."

"Wouldn't 'damp' be a little less affected?" Mrs. Munson asked me. She often applied the word "affected" to my work. I had looked it up. It meant phony and pretentious. She'd hurt my feelings, of course. Wasn't that what she was all about?

Fortunately, the bell rang before I could stammer a reply. Althea, Mitzie, and I kept our seats while everyone else bolted for the door. Woody knocked Sam Pendergast into the cork bulletin board and then kicked his feet out from under him.

"Hey, quit it!" Greg Thompson yelled at Woody, risking ending up on the floor with Sam. But Woody was already shoving his way through the door, his elbows jabbing and his thick black boots stomping on everybody's feet.

Sam waited in silence until most of the crowd disappeared before he got up and pushed his glasses back in place.

"You all right?" I asked him.

Sam shrugged wordlessly and hitched sideways out the door, all elbows and knees and misery. Mrs. Munson had seen what happened, but she'd left without even changing her surly expression.

We three girls looked at each other.

"What class do you have next?" I asked Althea.

"History, Room 202," she said, consulting her schedule. Her voice was quiet but surprisingly rough, as if she had a cold. Or had been crying. But her round dark eyes were clear.

"Mitzie and I have trig, down the hall," I told her. "Your room is at the other end of the second floor, Althea. You'd better hurry. I hope we see you later, maybe at lunch."

We pushed out into the hall and separated. The noise level was too great for conversation, so Mitzie and I hurried along, exchanging smiles and shrugs.

After we'd settled ourselves in trig, Jennifer and her two best friends sat down in the front row and whispered and giggled. Their thoughts were jagged, spraying from them like small bits of broken glass. Beside me, Mitzie sighed and pulled her dark hair down over her face. I thought that she was trying to hide at least a small part of herself. Jennifer and company made her miserable. Knowing that kept them happy.

I thought about the new girl again, making her way late to class, dressed in her weird clothes. There was something about her, something new and unscarred, that was certain to attract attention.

Greg Thompson skidded in, almost late again. He bent down beside me and said, "Hey, how about the new girl? I like her." Then he threw himself into his seat behind Mitzie, pawed his curly brown hair with a big, square hand, and grinned obligingly. "Are you working in the store tomorrow? I am."

I didn't have a chance to answer, because the teacher began writing on the board and talking.

Okay, Althea had three friends. That was a start.

At lunch, after Mitzie and I had begun eating at our usual corner table, we saw Althea come into the cafeteria. Silence enveloped the room as she slowly walked through it. She looked around as if she was studying faces.

"I'll ask her to sit with us," I told Mitzie and the other girls and I got up so quickly that I nearly spilled my milk.

Althea saw me and waited. "There's room at our table," I said. "Unless you're meeting someone. . . ."

"Thank you," she murmured in her strange, hoarse voice. I introduced her around, although two of the girls already knew her from morning classes. She nodded at everyone, then folded her hands on her pocketbook.

"Aren't you going to eat?" Julie asked.

"I'm not hungry," Althea said.

I pushed my bag of grapes toward her. "Would you like some?"

"No, thank you, Bridget," she said, carefully polite.

While we ate, she looked around the cafeteria slowly, studying faces again.

"Are you looking for somebody?" Mitzie asked. "Can we help you find someone?"

"No, thank you," Althea said.

Mitzie held a chocolate chip cookie out to her. "Try this. Mom makes the best."

Althea shook her head wordlessly.

Mitzie shrugged and offered the cookie to me.

"Yum," I said, taking it.

After a while Mitzie and Julie began telling jokes, and I nearly forgot Althea. When I looked back at her, she was sitting erect but her eyes were closed. I wouldn't have been surprised to see tears running down her face. She gave off waves of grief, a high, cold tide of it.

"Are you all right?" I asked.

Althea's black eyes opened abruptly. For a moment I was frightened out of my senses, because what I saw in her eyes was so terrible. Water and darkness and an awful fall, down and down, and a mother's anguish.

"I'm fine, thank you," Althea said. "I need to find a restroom."

"Go out the main cafeteria door and turn right," Mitzie said. "Do you want company?"

Althea shook her head, gathered up her pocketbook, and excused herself. When she was out of hearing, Mitzie said, "I think she's crying."

"Poor kid," Julie said. "Being new in school is rotten. And she has funny clothes. But I'm crazy about her hair. It makes me feel like petting it."

We all laughed. Julie was homely and freckled, but she was so sweet, like Mitzie. That was the nicest thing I could say about anyone, that she was as sweet as Mitzie.

Althea turned up again in my last period art class. The teacher sent her to the drawing board in the back corner, between the last window and the supply cupboards. She sat next to Jordan O'Neal. Jordan and all the kids on that side of the room were juniors, but there was no room left for Althea on the lowly sophomore side.

I wished I sat by Jordan. I saw him bending over his drawing board, never looking up no matter what. He was the saddest person I'd ever known.

"Bridget?" Miss Ireland asked.

My head jerked around. "Yes?"

She was standing next to me, smiling. She'd been talking to me, but I'd been gawking at Jordan as if I'd never seen him before. I felt that way every time I saw him.

"Will you finish your watercolor in time for the art fair?" she asked.

"I've got enough time," I said.

Miss Ireland smiled again. "I've put aside a mat for you. Just tell me when you want it."

I was dazzled by her attention and afraid my work wouldn't live up to her expectations.

"I saw your aunt last night," she said. "She's so proud of you."

I grinned, pleased.

Miss Ireland moved on. She stopped by Greg Thompson's desk to admire his drawing and laugh at something he said. He was a clown, but he was the best artist in school. I was second best, thanks to the encouragement I'd had from Miss Ireland and my aunt. They acted as if they thought I was wonderful.

Most of the time I felt as if I were on a speeding bus that didn't have a driver. If I hadn't had Aunt Cait, I wouldn't have known what to do. I could tell her what I thought about anything and not worry about ridicule or blame. Unfortunately, our friendship was one of the things that drove my mother crazy.

Sometimes—but not often—I wished I could be like Jennifer Budd, for the safety it would bring. Oh, to be what everyone expected teenage girls to be, vain, shallow, noisy, and sneaky. Then no one would bother asking me what I was thinking. And if anyone did, I'd be sly enough to make something up.

I looked out the window and saw that a mist had

drifted through the trees on the school lawn. It collected on colored leaves and dripped slowly, glimmering in the golden afternoon light. Half a dozen tree spirits bathed their small pointed faces in it, and when they saw me watching, they flickered their opal wings and disappeared within the shelter of the peach and gold leaves.

Summer was over.

I felt the stranger, Althea, staring at me, and startled, I met her dark gaze.

She knows, I thought. She knows about me. But I couldn't know about her, because she'd learned to shut everyone out. And that was a very strange thing.

I tried to concentrate on the exercise in perspective Miss Ireland had given us, but my mind wandered. I doodled small figures on the corner of my paper, the little tree spirits I'd seen bathing their faces.

"I know them from somewhere," Miss Ireland said. She was back at my elbow again, smiling while she studied the winged spirits. "Have you drawn them before?"

She startled me and I didn't think before I acted, so I turned to look out the window at the nearest tree, where I'd seen the spirits.

"Oh!" she said, flushing as if she was guilty of something. She moved on and didn't glance back.

I stared after her, embarrassed. She probably believed I was crazy.

She stopped to talk to Jordan. He liked painting more

than drawing, and lately all he'd been drawing in class was his old dog that had died during the summer. No matter what the assignment, Jordan drew Mikey. Things were bad at his house.

Althea held a pencil lightly while she looked out the window at the colorless sky. Greg Thompson laughed at something the boy next to him said. Mitzie cleared her throat, then coughed. She was allergic to eraser dust.

Art was my favorite class. I bent over my paper and added another bathing tree spirit to the cluster I'd drawn at the edge of my paper.

The bell rang, and I took a deep breath. Time to start home.

Althea was the first one out of the room, gone before I could call out, her skirt and hair fluttering behind her. I'd wanted to talk to her when we'd have more time, find out where she lived, and try to make friends.

I didn't know why I had goosebumps on my arms.

~❧~

chapter Two

$\mathcal{M}$itzie and I dawdled home under trees tangled in streamers of fog. Other kids from school appeared and disappeared in the drifting mist, their voices curiously muffled. By twos and threes, they turned off at corners or disappeared behind fences and hedges. Mitzie and I lived farther away, so after half a mile, we were nearly alone in that mysterious world of muted sounds and suddenly looming and disappearing houses and trees.

We were alone except for Jordan, of course. He walked behind us the way he usually did, head down, keeping company only with his thoughts.

Mitzie and I discussed Mrs. Munson, Jennifer, and Woody. Always, they provoked us to both anger and laughter. We'd been sophomores for three weeks, and we hated school for the first time in our whole lives. Mrs. Munson was the main reason.

Every morning I promised myself that I'd be perfect in her class that day and she'd change her mind about me before the bell rang for the next class, and every day I left her room with a knot in my stomach, a burning face, and a desire to scream. Nothing good that happened the rest of the day ever made up for the bad start. Mitzie said she felt the same way.

Add Jennifer and Woody to Mrs. Munson, and that made a nightmare. I'd tried a couple of times to discuss this with my parents, but they'd said I should handle my troubles with bullies and nasty teachers myself. I should learn to live with them, they'd said, agreeing with each other for once. At least Mitzie's parents sympathized with her.

I should have known how to fix my problems, but worry stole confidence from me. I needed to talk to my aunt.

But if I did, then wouldn't she remind me again that turning my back on my nature only hurt me?

"You know you have gifts like mine, like your great-grandmother's," she'd said many times. "We have them for a reason. Denying them weakens you, and when you're weak, you attract trouble."

I hadn't seen her very often before I moved to Bay-head. I remembered her only as the nice relative who brought me books and toys. Once she'd stood up for me when I'd begun talking about the earth spirit who lived in the vacant lot across the street and Mom snapped at me to be quiet. Mom hated hearing me talk about that mystical world I knew when I was little, the world she never saw. Finally I learned the hard lesson of silence, silence, and gradually most of that other world paled to invisibility.

Until I moved to Bayhead and began visiting my aunt.

One day Aunt Cait had simply asked, "Do you remember the earth spirit in Seattle, the one you knew when you were five?"

When I nodded, she asked me if I ever saw beings like that in Bayhead.

Of course I had. I knew the earth spirits in the fields and the tree spirits in every tree I saw.

I had shaken my head in a lie that day, but Cait had brushed back my hair and said, "Don't deny your powers. You're special. There are reasons . . ."

But I'd cried and said, "I don't want to be different. I want to be like everybody else."

Only I wasn't.

Mitzie interrupted my brooding. "I'll tell you what," she said as she shifted her backpack to one shoulder. "I'm sorry for Althea. Did you see how Jennifer looked at her?"

"She was sizing her up to find the best place to stab her with a poisoned dart," I said.

"It doesn't pay to be different," Mitzie said. "Not even a little bit. There are insiders and outsiders, and Althea's going to be an outsider."

"She's in good company," I said. "Wouldn't you rather be friends with Julie and Mary Anne, instead of Jennifer and her stuck-up friends?"

"You bet!" Mitzie said. "But I wish I'd had the chance to dump Jennifer just once. Hey, I wonder where Althea comes from."

"I'll bet she's not from anywhere around Seattle," I said. Bayhead was a small town north of Seattle, and the city influenced it. Althea would have attracted stares in Seattle, too.

We'd passed the place where the sidewalks ended, walking between maples that spread their branches across the road and shed yellow leaves on us. The last migrating birds had already flown south, and the songbirds that were left were the ones that hung around the houses that had bird feeders. Mitzie's house had six. We had only two, so I fed birds on the ground.

I also took seeds out to the edge of the woods behind Jordan's house for the quail, because they were afraid of our dog. Even when Jordan's dog, Mikey, was still alive, Jordan and I had fed the quail there, although his dog was old and seldom left his porch. He died all alone one day when Jordan was mowing lawns on the other side of town. I helped Jordan bury the poor old fellow, because his father didn't come home that night.

When we reached Mitzie's driveway, she said, "Come in and share the last of the coconut cake with me."

"I can't," I said. "Bingo's been shut up all day. I hate making him wait to go out."

Mitzie waved good-bye and I walked a little faster. The fog was thinning out, and I saw sunlight farther down the road. Sometimes Jordan caught up with me after I left Mitzie, and I glanced back to see if he was behind me. Yes. I slowed down again, hoping I wasn't too obvious.

"Hey, Bridget," Jordan said when he'd reached my side. "I got a sack of cracked corn at the feed store last night. The quail should like it."

I nodded and decided to take a big chance. "Come home with me while I let Bingo out. We can have hot chocolate before we feed the quail." I pretended great interest in two Steller's jays watching us from a crooked old apple tree where copper-colored apples still hung among the yellowing leaves.

"I'd better not," Jordan said. He pushed his dark hair away from his forehead. "I need to talk to Dad before he goes out."

Jordan's father hadn't worked for months. I didn't know what he did during the day, but he left nearly every afternoon and stayed away nearly every night.

"How is your dad?" I asked, deliberately cheerful. Mr.

O'Neal was supposed to be suffering from depression, but mostly he was just a drunk, and I couldn't feel sorry for him. He and my father weren't friends, even though they lived across the street from each other.

"Hey, there's the new girl," Jordan said suddenly.

That was a convenient change of subject, I thought. But Althea was two long country blocks ahead of us. She walked close to the edge of the road, near the ditches and hedges, and because of the color of her clothes and hair, she was nearly invisible against the autumn foliage.

"Let's talk to her," I said.

"Too late," Jordan said. "She's practically even with my driveway already."

He was right. "Poor girl," I said. "Woody gave her a hard time in first period."

"Woody," Jordan said disgustedly.

He stopped. I stopped. "I'll let Bingo out and come over," I said. I'd already seen that his dad's truck wasn't there. He'd left for wherever he went when he should have been at a job or at home with his son. Jordan wouldn't be able to have that talk.

"Yeah, sure," Jordan said. His eyes were blue, but not the same blue as mine. His were nearly green. Mitzie had said that he was the best-looking boy in school, but no one noticed because he was so quiet. He'd lived in Bayhead for two years, and I wondered if he'd spoken to more than a dozen kids that whole time.

19

I blinked and turned my face to make myself stop staring. My big old house was across the street, nearly hidden behind a laurel hedge, but somehow Bingo knew I was there, so he'd begun barking.

"Bingo wants out in a hurry," Jordan said, grinning. I couldn't help but think of Mikey and how he had waited for Jordan every afternoon.

"See you in a minute," I said as I swallowed tears.

Jordan loped up his driveway, which ran between a yellowed lawn and a fence overgrown with dying wild vines. Sorrow sifted over me.

I saw Althea even farther away then, near the fork in the road, and I expected her to turn left, toward the new development. Instead, she turned right and started up the long, steep road. But no one lived on the cliff, not since the first of the big spring mud slides. One house had tumbled down to the rocks then, and the other house had been condemned. I hadn't gone there since, because the ground was too unstable. I had a bad feeling about the place. I didn't even like to look up at it when I was walking on the Puget Sound beaches south of Bayhead.

I stopped at my front walk and watched Althea disappear among the trees. Strange. Where was she going?

The fairy moss rose rustled when I passed on my way to the porch. Oblivious to thorns, the frog crouched beneath the leaves, watching me. His brilliant green skin looked wet. His small black eyes were attentive. I knew better than to stop, but I did. He shouldn't have been there. Probably, I thought, he really *wasn't* there. But all my life he had charmed me at the same time he exasperated me, so in spite of my intentions, I said, "What now?"

"You're welcome to stay out here with me," xiii said. His name, he'd said, was pronounced *shhh*. "I'm better company than that big-mouthed, stupid dog, of course." He interrupted himself to stare at a small brown insect struggling over a dead leaf.

"Don't," I said hastily. "Not while I'm watching."

"Then don't watch," xiii said. His tongue flicked out, and when he swallowed, he blinked his eyes the way real frogs did.

My stomach heaved painfully and I wished that xiii wouldn't eat in front of me. Not that he cared what I thought. I couldn't have been more than three the first time I saw him eat, and I'd run crying into the house.

"You're disgusting," I said as I walked away.

Behind me, xiii laughed. "Why do you insist on believing that everything you see is real?" he asked. "Or that everything you dream isn't?"

Bingo was howling. By the time I unlocked the door, he sounded as if he was being murdered.

I dropped my backpack and bent to scratch Bingo's neck and ears the way he liked. He wouldn't stand still very long but shot out the open door, leaped nimbly sideways when he passed xiii, and raced around the side of the house.

I tossed my bag and jacket on the couch and took the note off the mantel. There was a note every time Mom drove into Seattle.

"Laundry," the note said on the first line. Then, "Start dinner. Spaghetti okay."

The mantel clock struck a quarter to four. I wouldn't have much time to spend with Jordan.

Bingo rushed back into the house and jumped up on me, leaving muddy paw marks on my jacket. He had a strand of blackberry vine caught in his long brown hair, and I pulled it out carefully. He smiled, panted, slobbered on me, and then ran to the kitchen. I heard him drinking water.

I hurried to get the first load of laundry in the washer.

Jordan and I shared an ancient cedar stump at the edge of a clearing in the woods, sitting close together in the mist-drenched afternoon, waiting for the quail. The stump was wet, and my jeans were cold and clammy.

I came alone each morning at first light and scattered seeds near the brambles where the quail hid. I couldn't wait for them to come out then, but I had time in the afternoons. And waiting gave me a chance to sit with Jordan.

"They're late," he whispered.

"They'll come," I whispered back.

Jordan looked over his shoulder at me. "I shouldn't wait much longer. My dad might come back, and I don't want to miss him."

I nudged him, liking the feeling I got when I touched his jacket. "Just a few more minutes."

His dad wouldn't come back, not for hours, if at all. What was going to happen to Jordan? I knew his mother had died when he was small. If he had relatives besides his father, he'd never mentioned them.

I didn't like his father. He wasn't cruel like Woody. He was weak and self-pitying. I'd given up saying hello to him, because he never answered but only shifted his gaze and tried not to see me so he wouldn't have to bother becoming involved with a neighbor.

Jordan was a junior. Next year he'd graduate and then he'd be gone. I already felt lost and forgotten.

Jordan drew a breath, ready to whisper again, but at that moment the first quail crept out from the shelter of the brambles. It was the largest male. He froze for a moment, his plump gray-and-tan body nearly invisible against the brush. Then he advanced one step and stopped again. He turned his head from side to side, searching for danger. His little black topknot quivered.

In that moment, I was aware of the sharp scent of wet cedars and ferns in the damp forest, and Jordan's clean, soapy smell. I heard the faint sound of mist dripping in the trees around us. I felt the rough stump under my hand.

The quail stepped forward again, and then he waited. Jordan and I didn't move. Two more quail came out, then three more. They moved soundlessly to the cracked corn and bird seed. The largest male didn't eat, but watched, watched, until the rest were finished. Only then did he gobble up the last of the meal.

Jordan and I relaxed. We'd done this every afternoon for weeks, even in the rain. The lives of the quail had been hard since so much of the forest and fields had been sacrificed for the new houses. There were several cats in the neighborhood now. They'd caught most of the quail chicks hatched in July. My parents thought I was foolish for trying to keep the poor birds alive.

"Learn to accept these things," they had told me. "Why are you always fighting the inevitable?"

"The chicks were a gift," Cait had said. "Celebrate their mortal lives and then cry and let go. Bridget, listen! You'll see them again and you know it!"

"Stop whining over your nightmares," xiii had snapped. "If you won't take good advice, don't expect *me* to feel sorry for you. Don't I have enough work around here?"

I was getting stiff from the chill, sitting there on the damp stump. Suddenly I felt compelled to look up.

Through the thinning mist, I saw the silhouettes of three falcons.

Jordan saw them, too. I heard him gasp.

The quail cried out their sharp alarm calls and burst into low flight, wings beating, heading toward the trees.

The falcons circled over the clearing once and then vanished into the mist. It wasn't a good afternoon for hunting, and they couldn't pursue the quail through the thick woods where there was no room to maneuver.

"They were peregrines, I think," Jordan whispered.

I thought so, too, even though I'd never seen them that far from the cliff before or showing interest in birds on the ground.

The quail fell silent in the woods. I blessed them as well as I could, even though my heart was still beating so hard and fast that I could scarcely think. I tried to surround them with the circle of bright protection that I'd known how to cast all my life, but I was too nervous to do a proper job. It took a lot of confidence to cast a proper circle, and it had been a while since I had been strong enough. It had been since school started.

No, that's not true, I thought. It had been since I decided to fight off my nature, my own self.

"Let's go," Jordan said, and he slid down from the stump. I followed, and my jeans felt even more clammy than before.

When we reached the fence that separated his backyard from the woods, Jordan jumped over it then waited to make sure I'd get over without snagging my pants the way I had once. He waved and disappeared through his back door where the paint was peeling and Mikey's old scratch marks still showed.

I was halfway through making dinner when Mom came home. She hurried into the kitchen even before she took off her suit jacket.

"Are you fixing a salad?" she asked.

Thanks, Mom, I thought. And how was *your* day?

"I made a big salad," I said. "It's in the refrigerator." I stirred the spaghetti sauce so that I had a reason not to look at her. "And I set the table and did two loads of laundry."

"The traffic was terrible," she said. "I don't know how much longer I can stand commuting all the way to Seattle. I still wish we hadn't moved here."

"At least you don't have to go into the city every day anymore," I said. "Since the merger, you've only had to work part-time." As soon as I spoke, I wondered if I'd lost my mind, but I couldn't stop myself from careening down this conversational hill and making everything worse. "You could quit and go to work at the store with Dad and Cait. You wouldn't have to drive—"

"I'd rather be dead than work in that garden store," she said. "I didn't spend six years in college so that I could wait on people."

"Right." I stirred the sauce again, hating myself for ever opening my mouth.

Dad came in, rubbing his hands together. "Do I smell the best spaghetti sauce in the whole world?"

"I made twice as much as we need," I told him. "I'll put some in the freezer."

He kissed Mom, patted my shoulder, and helped himself to a carrot. "John's out sick, so I'll have to go back to the store after dinner," he said.

Mom sighed. "Can't Cait . . ."

"Cait's coming in, too," Dad said. "We're pretty busy."

Mom excused herself to change her clothes, and Dad helped himself to cold water from the refrigerator. I told him about Jordan waiting for his father and then about the new girl at school.

"I think she lives in that house up on the cliff," I said as I dropped pasta into boiling water.

"I doubt that," Dad said. "The last I heard, the owners still can't get the condemnation order lifted, and they've been fighting the county for months."

"If it hasn't fallen off the cliff by now, then maybe it's not going to," I said.

Mom came back, buttoning a cotton shirt. "The

whole cliff will slide down into the Sound one of these days," she said. "That's what Cait says, and she should know. She's lived here since the year Dot."

"Oh, before that," Dad said soberly, but his eyes were laughing. "She was here before God made people, she says."

Cait was fifteen years older than Dad. She had practically raised him after their parents died. They were very close, and Mom didn't like it. In a way I didn't blame her. She must have felt left out sometimes. And it couldn't have been easy having a sister-in-law like Cait. Actually, Cait was nearly old enough to be her mother-in-law. I suspected that that made everything worse.

"You think someone is living in the house?" Mom asked me.

"I saw the new girl turning up the road."

"Maybe she was just going for a walk," Mom said. She took butter out of the refrigerator, stepped over sleeping Bingo, and put it on the table.

"Maybe," I said doubtfully. I stirred the sauce once more and splattered it on my shirt.

After dinner, I let Bingo out the front door for his evening run and watched while he dodged xiii, who was squatting on the bottom step.

I slipped out and closed the door behind me.

"What are you doing on the porch?" I demanded.

"Waiting for you," xiii said. "Trouble's coming."

"Thanks," I said bitterly. I didn't need this weird creature predicting my future. "Aren't you supposed to be hibernating? We learned in science class that frogs bury themselves in mud after the weather gets cold."

"Thanks for reminding me," xiii said, sounding cranky. He made a little grunting sound then popped into the form I saw him in most often. He was a thin boy, pale, with long red hair and slanted green eyes. He was small enough to sit on my palm, but I didn't touch him. A rattlesnake was safer.

He finger-combed his hair and smiled up at me, showing pointed teeth. "Satisfied?" he asked. "Satisfied, oh golden witch-child who denies her heritage and can't cast a decent circle to save her life? I know what happened out there in the woods. Disgraceful, if you ask me."

"Who asked you?" I cried, furious. Then, seeing him standing there naked, I added, "I wish you'd wear clothes. You embarrass me."

"I'm not cold," he said. "Your embarrassment doesn't interest me in the least."

I climbed the steps, but he scampered ahead of me, persistent. "Trouble's coming," he said again.

"What kind?" I asked. "School?"

Xiii touched one finger to his mouth, cocked his head, and considered my question. "I'm the threshold guardian, not your nursemaid," he said. "But you need to remember how to cast a circle properly."

And then he was gone. Blink—and he was gone.

Mom opened the door and said, "Who are you talking to?"

"Bingo," I lied as I shuffled inside. On cue, Bingo raced past us, panting, nearly knocking both of us down.

Later, when we were cleaning the kitchen, Mom asked if I planned to work in the store the next morning.

"Until one," I said as I loaded dishes into the dishwasher. "Then I thought I'd go over to see Cait. Miss Ireland wants me to enter my bird watercolor in the art fair, and I could use a little help."

"Miss Ireland is very talented," Mom said without looking up from the counter she was wiping. "Why don't you ask her for help?"

"She helps me every day," I said. "I want another viewpoint."

"Write down the date for the art fair on the calendar," Mom said. "I don't want to forget it. Who won last year?"

"Greg Thompson," I said as I started the dishwasher. "He'll win again."

"Don't be negative," Mom said. "You're always so negative, Bridget. Isn't Jordan in your art class, too?"

"Yes, but he only draws Mikey. Miss Ireland lets him."

"His father—" Mom began, and then she stopped.

"Well, I suppose a neglectful father is better than none at all."

Dad turned off the kitchen TV. "Did you remember to pay the light bill?" he asked Mom.

Mom stared at him. "I thought *you* were going to take care of it," she said.

Dad shrugged. "Oh well. It won't hurt if it's a little late."

"It's *always* a little late," Mom said.

I left before the familiar argument got louder, and I wondered how long it would be before our electricity was shut off for the third time.

The bus has no driver, I thought. What's going to happen to us? Dad had lost his city job, and Mom had been transferred to a part-time job she hated at the bank. All we had was the garden store that had belonged to my dead grandparents, and the old house.

Five minutes later, when I was upstairs in my room, I heard my parents laughing about something. I wondered if they had any idea how childish they were. Sometimes I even wondered if they were crazy. I knew that I was.

I pushed back my curtains and looked out into the dark. The last of the fog had blown away ahead of the wind that tore leaves from the trees and sent them streaming down the road. Overhead, a single star awoke and sleepily promised me a wish.

Cast a circle, xiii had said. Around myself? Around the quail? Around my parents?

Around Jordan?

I wish that we could all be safe, I thought.

Sorry, the star called out in its piping little voice. I don't recognize that wish.

Then I heard xiii laughing.

࿊

chapter Three

By ten o'clock Saturday, the sun had burned off the morning mist, and the sky was so bright a blue that I had to squint when I looked up. As I walked to work, I could have wished to spend the morning somewhere else, but I liked helping Dad out on weekends.

My family's garden store and the display yards around it always thrilled me when I caught my first glimpse of them half a block away. That morning the sight was better than usual. The trees, both the permanent ones and the ones Dad was selling, glowed red and yellow against the brilliant sky, and dozens of birds fluttered among the ornamental maples on the south side, where I could see Greg filling the bird feeders.

"Hey, Greg," I called out when I got close enough.

He turned around and made a great pretense of being angry. "You get to be late because you're the boss's daughter," he shouted.

I waited until I didn't have to yell to answer. "Mom let Bingo out right after I left, and he caught up with me, so I had to take him back. She forgets to give me enough time to get out of sight."

"Yeah," Greg said, and he made a sympathetic face. He knew that my mother often screwed things up accidentally on purpose. There's a relief in knowing and liking someone for a long time, even though there aren't many secrets left.

"She wanted me to help with the housework this morning," I said. I grabbed a feeder and held it while Greg poured seed inside.

"So you came here to do your dad's housework instead," he said. "But it's nicer housework."

He was right. I didn't mind sweeping the cement paths that led between the rows of trees and shrubs planted in big pots, waiting for buyers. I didn't even mind washing windows. And when I was done with those things, I'd spend the rest of my time in the shed with Greg, helping him pour bark into big plastic bags.

When we left, Greg would get a check and I'd get enough cash to buy myself a sandwich and a soda on my way home. It never occurred to Dad that I might like a paycheck instead of an allowance and lunch money.

I was nearly finished with the windows when Mitzie showed up, towing her little sister Anna.

"Will you be finished soon?" Mitzie asked. "I'm stuck with Anna for the day, and I thought we could have lunch and then go to the mall."

"I won't be done for another two hours," I said as I wiped water off the window next to the side door. "Then I'm going over to Cait's."

"Lucky you," Mitzie mourned. She loved my aunt.

"Let's go!" Anna demanded. Nine years old, she was a miniature of Mitzie, with rich curly hair and skin the color of cream. She already was showing signs of the family weight problem. "I don't want to hang around here."

"Say hello to Bridget," Mitzie said. "Don't be so rude."

"I'm always rude," Anna said truthfully, but she grinned at me. "Come on, come on, come on, Mitzie!"

Mitzie stood her ground. "Are you working with Greg today?" she asked me.

"He's around here somewhere," I said as I started work on another window.

"He's so funny. I like him."

"I'll be sure to tell him," I said, smirking.

Mitzie socked my arm. "Don't you dare. I was only making a comment. He's probably got a crush on you, not that it will do him any good."

"Do we have to talk about boys?" Anna demanded. "I want to go!"

After they left, I thought about what Mitzie had said. No, it wouldn't do Greg much good if he had a crush on me. I didn't have anything against him. He was funny. He was even cute. But there was Jordan, quiet, somber, lost.

I sighed and heard a fluttering sound behind me. When I turned, I saw a small gray bird clinging unsteadily to the branch of a potted cherry tree.

"Weren't you supposed to fly south?" I asked.

"Her wing is injured," a tree spirit called from her hiding place deep within the leaves. "What will she do when the winds come? Where will she go? When the winds come."

My eyes stung with unshed tears when I turned back to my work. Why couldn't I fix things? Why was there so much suffering in the world?

Poor bird. Poor Jordan.

"What's wrong, chickie?" Dad asked from the other side of the glass. He always called me chickie when Mom wasn't around.

"I think the bird in that tree is hurt," I said.

"It's got a good winter home here," he said. "Lots of them spend the nights on the rafters in the shed. We put out plenty of food. That little bird will make it through."

He walked off, smiling, certain that he had solved all my problems. I looked back at the bird. She clung, trembling, to her branch, too weak to fly to the shed even if she knew she'd find shelter there.

Dad also was a passenger on that bus that didn't have a driver, but he didn't seem to know. Or care. He wasn't like Jordan's dad, but he seemed unable to take real care of all the things he should, so . . . I struggled to think this traitorous thought all the way through. My father *said* all the right words. But he was—careless.

Greg, on the other hand, was not a passenger on a careening bus. It was a relief to find him waiting when I walked into the shed.

"Does your dad know that Christopherson's is selling bagged bark for a dollar less?" he asked as he handed me a plastic bag, which I promptly dropped.

"Probably not," I said. I bent to pick up the bag. "Why don't you tell him?"

"*You* tell him," he said. He scraped bark from the big container into the bag as I held it open.

"He won't listen. He'd have to change the signs."

"He's losing a lot of business to Christopherson's," Greg said as he stapled the bag shut. "They give a big discount if people buy all their lawn supplies there. They pass out flyers to the people in the new houses."

"He should hire you as his business manager," I said.

"Not me," Greg said. "I hate business. Hey, you want to go beachcombing when we're done here? There was a high tide last night, so the pickings ought to be better this time than they were the last time we went."

"I'm going over to my aunt's," I said.

"I'm madly in love with your aunt," he said as he heaved the sack on the pile that sat near the door. "I'd write poems to her but I'm afraid she'd laugh, since she's a published poet and famous and all that."

"She wouldn't laugh," I said, "But she might show them to your mother."

Greg looked up at me and grinned. Mitzie was right. He *was* cute, with curly brown hair and eyes as green as grass. "My mother thinks your aunt is a witch," he said.

His remark chilled me. "That's a rotten thing to say," I said.

"Get another sack, lazybones," he said. "No, it's not a rotten thing to say. I told Mom that I hoped Cait was a witch, because maybe she could sell me a potion that I could use on Woody to rid the world of him."

I held open a sack. "So what did your mom say?"

"She said that I should learn to get along with Woody," he said, and he laughed.

I shook my head and laughed, too. "They just don't get it," I said. "We *can't* get along with him. Well, maybe if we paid him money. I'd heard about him even when he was at North Hill Elementary and we were at Sunset Heights. I just never thought I'd have to put up with him."

"He wasn't so bad last year," Greg said.

"He had a cast on his leg most of last year!" I said. "He

kicked people and hurt them with his cast even more than he does with rotten old boots now."

"But we didn't have him in first period last year," Greg concluded. "I feel sorry for the new girl. What's her name? Althea. Yeah. There's something about her, I don't know, something really different. Woody will zero in on that. It's like chickens, you know. If one of them is hurt, the others pick on her."

"What makes you think Althea is hurt?" I asked.

Greg tossed another sack on the pile and brushed his hands off on his jeans. "I don't know. Not hurt, exactly. It's how she looks. Her clothes, maybe. Or her hair. It's something."

"I know," I said. "Like Jordan. I know his dad's a drunk and his mother's dead. But there's something even worse. It's like he's not even trying any more. I wish I could do something for him."

Greg straightened up and stretched his arms above his head. "You worry too much, especially about Jordan. He and his dad will move on to another place someday. You don't want to . . ." He stopped and looked away from me, as if he was embarrassed.

"I don't want to *what?*" I asked. I knew I was blushing.

He shrugged and shook his head, then looked back at me. "You worry too much," he repeated.

When Greg finished work and left, I saw him stop sud-

denly by the potted cherry tree. He carefully picked
something up from the ground, cradled it in his hand, and
walked away.

He's taking the injured bird home, I thought as I
watched.

"The boy, the boy," sang the tree spirits.

I smiled, knowing then that the bird would survive.

I ran home after I finished work, expecting to find Mom
out running errands. But she was sitting in the kitchen,
drinking coffee and paging through a magazine. The
breakfast dishes still sat on the table.

"I thought you were going shopping," I said as I patted
Bingo. I'd brought my sandwich and soda home with me,
and I offered her half of the sandwich.

She shook her head. "No, I don't like ham." She
looked back down at the magazine.

"*Are* you going shopping?" I asked, hating myself for
slipping into the trap.

"I thought we could both go," she said as she turned a
page.

"But I'm going over to Cait's," I said. "I told you
that."

She turned another page. "I forgot," she said, and she
sighed.

Bingo, hearing the sigh, hurried out of the room.

40

The bus was barreling downhill again.

"Well, I'll take my sandwich with me and eat over there," I said. "I'll get my portfolio and—"

"I hate it that you spend so much time with her," Mom said.

"So much time? I haven't seen her for two weeks."

Another page turned. Another sigh. "She's not a good influence."

I stepped straight into that trap, too. "Why not?" I asked.

She switched her gaze to the cupboard over the refrigerator. "She's a very peculiar woman," Mom said, as if a Fountain of Knowledge in the cupboard had just produced that gem.

Now it was my turn to sigh. "What's that supposed to mean?" I asked.

"All that talk about the environment and ecology and animals becoming extinct—it puts everyone off. The people around here don't want to hear about those things. She talks about them when she's working at the store—"

"Where people come in to replace some of the trees that have been cut down," I said.

She looked at me then, and once again I was impressed with how pale and cold her eyes could be when she was upset.

"See?" she said finally. "You're getting to be just like her."

41

"I learned about things like that in school," I said. "And in magazines and books."

"You have to get along in this world. . . ." she began.

"Excuse me," I said stiffly. "I have to leave now."

I ran upstairs, got my portfolio, and ran out of the house with Bingo on a leash, because Cait was always glad to see him. Mom would have let him out anyway, before I was out of sight.

Cait wasn't anybody's idea of how a witch should look. She was tall and large-boned, with short curly hair that was sometimes red and sometimes blond. She wore tunics made of beautiful fabric over loose trousers, and she owned more earrings and rings than anybody else I'd ever known. I saw her through her front window, hair blond this time, as I ran up the porch steps.

As soon as she opened the door, Bingo leaped up and pawed her peacock-colored silk tunic. "Here you are, sweetie," she said to him. "Floss and Jasper are waiting for you."

I barely had time to take off Bingo's leash before he leaped into the next room, where Cait's two old cats lay on a couch. He jumped up beside them and thrust his head between them. Both of them began licking his face. Bingo closed his eyes in ecstasy.

"Come into the studio," Cait said. "I'll make tea and we'll have a look at your watercolor."

I followed her into the large room that held her work tables and her piano. In front of the window, Cait had set her table with fragile china cups and saucers. I put my portfolio on the work table under the skylight and took my usual chair. I'd left my lunch home, but I wasn't sorry. I was hungry, and I could see the platter of tea sandwiches sitting by the electric kettle in the small kitchen corner.

"Don't get comfortable yet," Cait said. "While I'm working, get out your watercolor and hold it up for me to see and think about."

I did as she asked, wondering what she'd say.

"Interesting," she said after studying it for a moment. "I see what you're doing. You have a panel for each of the seasons, and I think I recognize that bit of fence. Isn't it along the road north of your house?"

I nodded.

Cait poured a little boiling water from the kettle into the pot, shook it around, then poured it into the sink. I watched while she quickly added loose tea leaves, filled the pot with boiling water, and put on the lid.

"Now I can take a better look," she said. She stepped out from behind the narrow counter that separated the immaculate kitchen from the rest of the room. I held the painting as steady as I could.

"Nice," she said. "I like what you've done with winter. The owl is wonderful. Then spring, with a robin perched on the same fence. I like his eye. He looks alive. Summer and a quail, with every feather showing. That's beautiful, Bridget. But fall. Hmm. It's a nice wash. Lots of muted color, and you did the fog in the trees so well. But what bird are you going to put on the fence? The pencil outline looks almost like a small owl."

"I thought I'd put a hawk there, using a dry brush. Or maybe a peregrine falcon. I've seen them around again."

Cait looked up. "What happened to them last spring was terrible, losing their scrape with two fledglings in it. Well, I'm glad they're back. I've got some good snapshots of them, the ones I took last summer. Would you like to borrow them? I've got a couple of nice snapshots of that old redtail hawk who hangs around here teasing the cats every winter. Want to see them, too?"

"After tea," I said. I put my watercolor away and sat down again. "Is it ready yet?"

She brought the pot to the table and set it down in front of me. "You pour," she said.

I picked up the pot and the silver tea strainer, and filled her cup. Outside the window, a shower of leaves fell from the birch trees, even though there was no wind.

The color of the leaves reminded me of Althea. "There's a new girl in school," I said. "Her name is Althea. I feel sorry for her because she's dressed all wrong and her hair—well, it's wonderful in a way, but it's really

44

strange. And so is she. Really strange, I mean. She doesn't talk much, but she's always looking around, as if she's waiting for someone. Just—waiting."

Cait had sat down and lifted her teacup, but she seemed to freeze then. She stared at me. Her eyes were the same color as the antique gold coins hanging from her earlobes.

"Where does she come from?" she asked. "You must find out before you make friends with her."

"Why?" I asked, astonished. "What difference does it make?"

Cait blinked and shook her head. "Bridget, please think carefully. You don't know who she is, you don't know where she comes from, and she acts strangely. When *you* think someone's acting strangely, that means you need to look into her mind to see what she's hiding. We've talked about this sort of thing before."

I remembered how I had tried to look into Althea's mind when I first saw her, and how she had shut me out. But if I told Cait about that, she'd start in again on the gifts she and I shared, inherited from her grandmother, and never wasted until I began denying them. I didn't want the afternoon spoiled. Most of all, I didn't want to do what she wanted me to do.

"I'll try, Cait," I said, not meaning it but knowing that one witch couldn't read another's mind unless she allowed it—and I wasn't about to allow it. I concentrated hard on my hunger, just in case. "I'll really try, but right now I'm too hungry to think straight. Can't we eat?"

She paused, then picked up the platter of sandwiches and held it out to me. "I made your favorite, egg salad. There's ham, too. And a few cream cheese with green olives mixed in. If you don't eat them all, I'll be stuck with eating them for dinner."

We forgot about Althea then. We spent another hour over tea, gossiping. Then she showed me the plans she was drawing for the landscaping at the new library. I was sorry to leave. I was always sorry to leave her.

At home, xiii waited by the path, crouched under the moss rose.

"Did you learn anything from her?" he asked, crabby and determined to be as disagreeable as possible.

I stopped beside him. Bingo sat down, eyes averted from xiii. "Learn from Cait?" I asked. "What should I learn?"

"How to cast a decent circle, for one thing!" he cried. "You seem to have forgotten. You should be careful these days. How many times must I tell you that trouble's coming. Trouble is *coming!* You'd know that yourself if you weren't stubborn and stupid."

He was so upset and angry that he began changing form without control. The frog dissolved into a lump that wadded itself into a mouse, first green then brown, and then shifted and reformed, first into a white parrot and then a gray lizard, which sprouted wings and grew into a small silver dragon, which in turn seemed about to become even larger.

"Stop it!" I cried.

"It's *your* fault!" he yelled. "You're making me crazy!"

Bingo whined and tried to inch away from both of us, but the leash held him in place.

I studied xiii. "Who *are* you, really?" I asked.

"Why does it matter?" xiii asked irritably as he settled into his frog self. He brushed silver dragon scales off his legs.

"I've never actually known if you're a friend or an enemy," I said slowly, reluctantly. All my life, no matter where I'd lived, he'd been there, and I'd never been certain I could trust him completely.

Xiii laughed. "It's a little late for that," he said. He eyed a spider and flicked out his tongue.

"Ugh," I said, and I turned away.

Xiii blinked, swallowed, and said, "That boy's father won't come home."

I scowled. "Now you tell me. Are you sure?"

"Be careful," xiii said. "Trouble's coming."

"You keep saying that!" I cried. "But you never say what kind!"

But xiii was gone, leaving behind only a scattering of silver scales and a bit of the leg of the hapless spider.

Bingo whined and pulled at the leash. He wanted to go inside.

Mom wasn't home. It was nearly time to start dinner, so I took lasagna out of the freezer and turned on the oven. The breakfast dishes were still on the table.

I let Bingo lick them clean before I put them in the dishwasher.

chapter Four

Jordan was more silent than usual when we went to the woods to feed the quail that afternoon. I didn't ask about his father because I was afraid he still hadn't come home. Jordan didn't volunteer anything about him.

The quail crept out of the brush by twos and threes, ate their evening meal, and vanished silently back into hiding. I felt time slipping by, out of my control, and I longed to remember even one of the comments I was capable of thinking up in the middle of some of my sleepless nights. On our way out of the woods, I tried to invent a reason to invite Jordan to my house—or invite myself inside his. Nothing logical or believable occurred to me. Even in my mind, I stuttered and stammered. Hopeless.

Finally, out of a desperation that must have been obvious, I said, "Is everything okay, Jordan?"

He looked away from me, back toward the woods. "Sure. Sure. How's Bingo?"

The question was so unexpected that I burst out laughing.

"Bingo? What's wrong with you, Jordan?"

His mouth tightened. "Nothing's wrong. Hey, see you later, okay?"

He ran to his porch without glancing back even once, leaving me to mentally kick myself all the way home. Not for the first time, I wondered why I couldn't learn not to blab the first thing that came to my mind.

Xiii, dangling from a branch of a dogwood tree by one skinny arm and combing his long red hair with his free hand, hummed over my head.

"Don't talk to me," I said. I didn't stop walking.

"I'll leave the talking to *you,*" he said, snickering. "You do such a good job of it."

"Oh shut up," I muttered.

"What class! What style!" he crowed. "Jordan's father isn't coming home, you know. Or you *would* know, if you weren't so stubborn. Your powers—"

I shut the front door behind me with more force than necessary and startled Bingo, yelping, out of his nap.

* * *

After dinner, Mom and Dad left for a party, and Bingo and I went upstairs to eat popcorn and watch old movies in my bedroom.

I couldn't concentrate. Had Jordan's father come home yet? I couldn't see their house from my window unless I opened it and leaned out. My curiosity embarrassed me, but I had to know!

I shoved open my window and leaned out as far as I dared. I saw Jordan's lights, but the yard was dark, and if his father's truck was there, I couldn't see it.

Overhead, thin clouds blew across the full moon, and the air smelled of trees and water and the coming winter. Below, xiii, as a watchful dragon, stretched out on the path between the porch and the road. His silver scales gleamed. He twitched in his sleep and finally snored.

But then he jerked awake, his long neck stretched up, and his horned, horselike head turned first in one direction and then another. I knew he heard something, even though I couldn't. While I watched, he froze and then faded, until he was barely visible but glimmering like stardust. Behind me on the bed, Bingo raised his head.

A coyote trotted nervously down the road, tail down, ears pricked up. As he drew close to our yard, xiii snorted a blast of smoke tinged with pink fire in his direction. The coyote leaped sideways into the brush across the street. Xiii settled back down, flapped his stiff tail twice, and sighed.

"Bully," I called down.

He raised his head and snorted pink fire at me. "Tonight you'll dream true," he said. "And it serves you right. Now let me sleep."

I slammed the window down and pulled the curtains closed.

Probably I was going crazy, I thought. I would have been certain of it if Bingo hadn't run off when xiii scared away the coyote.

I shut off my TV when I heard my parents return. After a while, when the house was silent again, I fell asleep.

Or I thought I did.

In my dream, I felt drawn to the window again, and I leaned out into the dazzle of moonlight and starshine. Without a thought, I pulled on the gold velvet robe Cait had given me for my birthday, a garment so elegant that I had never worn it. Then, barefoot, I walked downstairs and left the house. Bingo didn't follow. Xiii was nowhere around.

I padded across the street and around the side of Jordan's dark house, certain of my destination. If the night was cold, I didn't feel it. I couldn't stop smiling.

But then I saw him, Jordan. He sat on the big rock we had rolled over Mikey's grave to keep wild things from digging him up. Jordan's head was bent, his face hidden in his hands.

He didn't hear me.

I walked up behind him and rested my hand on his shoulder. He looked up. I saw the marks of tears on his face.

"Jordan," I whispered. "It's all right. Come with me. I'll show you where Mikey is."

I held out my hand, and he took it and followed me. I led him to the fork in the road, and we climbed easily until we reached the cliff.

"There he is," I said, and I pointed out into the night, where we saw all the stars that had ever been, close to us, immediate, and barely out of reach. But still, they *were* out of reach, because this might not have been a dream after all.

"I can't see him," Jordan whispered.

I curled my arm around his shoulder and leaned against him. "Yes, you can," I whispered back, my lips close to his neck. "He's there, see? See him? He's young again, Jordan."

Jordan made a sound, almost a cry of pain, and I knew that he saw his dog. He watched Mikey run among the stars until the moon slid down the sky.

Jordan pressed his face against my hair and I turned up my mouth to his. "Bridget," he whispered against my lips.

Confused, I tried to turn away, but we were lost between swiftly fading stars, until Mikey, running ahead of us, showed us a way we had not seen before, a way that rose straight into a silver dawn.

"Now," xiii whispered at my ear. "Now, tell me what is true and what is not."

I sat up in bed, gasping, pressing my hands against my mouth.

"Leave me alone!" I whispered.

I left the house just after the sun came up, and even though Jordan never went to the woods with me in the mornings, I still dawdled through his backyard, hoping he'd know I was there, at the same time that I hoped he'd never know what I had dreamed.

Alone in the strangely silent woods, I put out seed for the quail. A hawk or a falcon must be nearby, I thought, because it seemed as if there was nothing small and feathered and gentle anywhere. I went home without waiting for the quail to come out. Jordan's house could have been deserted. The driveway was still empty.

Xiii slept curled under a leaf at the base of the moss rose. I was tempted to nudge him awake with my sneaker, but I left him alone and went inside for breakfast.

That afternoon I phoned Mitzie to see if she wanted company, but she was getting ready to leave.

"I'm going to Grandma's this afternoon, remember?" she said. "Listen, you'll never guess who I saw this morning when Mom and I went to the drugstore. Althea! She was standing in the Harrison Avenue Park, watching some kids play soccer. I thought about walking over to talk to her, but she's so weird, Bridget. And some of the boys were laughing at her. She was wearing the same clothes, even though she must have been freezing. She didn't have a jacket, either."

"She's really strange, but I still feel sorry for her," I said.

"She'll wear something different tomorrow, and then she won't look so funny," Mitzie said.

"Nobody will forget what she wore Friday," I said as I propped the phone between my shoulder and my ear so that I could rub my arms. "Nobody ever forgets anything."

"You mean Jennifer never forgets," Mitzie said bitterly.

"She's worse when she's in Munson's class," I said. "In Munson's class and in the cafeteria."

There was a small silence, and then Mitzie said, "You're right. But she was awful almost everywhere last year."

"So was Woody, even if he had a cast on his leg. Greg and I were talking about it yesterday. I wish I had enough nerve to pay Woody back just once."

Mom walked through the living room and gave me a look that meant she wanted me to hang up.

"Greg is so adorable that I dream about him," Mitzie said. "But I dream about half the boys in our class."

Without wanting to, I remembered my own dream, and I blushed so hard that my eyes burned. "Yes," I said vaguely.

Mom gestured from the dining room door.

"I've got to go," I told Mitzie. "See you tomorrow morning."

"If I live through Grandma's dinner," Mitzie said and hung up.

I'd barely replaced the phone when Mom said, "Dad told me he was coming home early for dinner this afternoon, but I have to pick up a few things at the store first. Can I count on you to help out?"

"Sure," I said nervously. What was coming next?

"I just wanted to make sure you weren't going over to Cait's again."

I shook my head. "No. I thought I might go over to Mitzie's, but she's leaving for—"

"Weren't you talking to Cait?"

"No, Mom," I said. Did she actually think I'd talk to Cait like that? "I was talking to Mitzie."

"You confide in Cait too much," Mom said, and she walked away before I could argue.

It was my turn to sigh.

Maybe people who eavesdrop don't always hear right.

Jordan didn't come out to feed the quail that evening.

That night, I was afraid I'd dream again, so I lay awake for hours, and when I slept at last, only tree spirits wandered with me in strange and beautiful forests.

* * *

The quail were waiting for me the next morning, so I
didn't have to worry about them all day. The woods were
filled with birds. And when I got home, all xiii said was,
"Good morning." Some days started out right. And
sometimes I didn't have enough sense to question luck.

I rarely saw Jordan walking to school, but that morning
I did. He was blocks ahead, and I made no effort to catch
up. I didn't think I could face him.

Mitzie entertained me with an account of dinner at
her grandmother's, and I was in an exceptionally fine
mood when we walked into first period.

I should have known. I should have heard the noise and
been prepared. But I was still laughing at Mitzie's descrip-
tion of soggy dumplings.

Althea sat rigidly in her seat, staring straight ahead,
while Woody and his friends tossed her pocketbook back
and forth. When it finally fell, Jennifer reached it first.
Laughing—shrieking, really—she kicked it.

It stopped, open and empty, at my feet.

chapter Five

I picked up Althea's empty pocketbook and looked around on the floor. "Where's her stuff?" I asked the kids watching me.

"What stuff?" Woody asked, smirking.

"Did you take her things out of her pocketbook?" I asked him.

He shook his head, smiling the way he did when he knew he was driving somebody crazy.

Jennifer's eyes glittered as she watched. She should have helped Althea instead of hurting her! She was a girl! A scalding bubble of anger burst inside me.

"Where are Althea's things?" I demanded.

She shrugged and smiled. "How should I know?"

Althea got up from her desk and took her pocketbook out of my hand. "Thank you, Bridget," she said.

"But it's empty," I said.

She hesitated, then said, "It doesn't matter," as she returned to her seat.

"Hey," I said, looking around. "Come on, everybody. What happened to her the rest of her things?"

"Yes," Mitzie said angrily. "You guys, give her back her stuff."

The smiles on the kids' faces faded a little. A couple of them looked around, puzzled.

Greg pushed between two of the boys. "They never stopped throwing her pocketbook around until you got here," he told me. "Nobody reached into it, and I didn't see anything fall out of it."

"Why didn't *you* help her, Greg?" I demanded.

"I tried," Greg said angrily. "I tried, and so did Sam and Julie. We couldn't catch it."

"We couldn't catch it," mimicked Woody. He folded his arms over his chest and smiled that smile I hated so much.

Mrs. Munson, behind her desk, called out, "Sit down, everybody. Sit down, Bridget! Don't start anything!"

I opened my mouth to protest, but Woody said, "Yeah, don't start anything, Bridget."

I felt as if I was firing off sparks. "Shut up, Woody!" I yelled. "You just shut your big mouth for once!"

He moved toward me, light on his feet, menacing.

"What did you say?" he asked softly.

"Shut up! Shut up! Give Althea back her things and

then shut your big stupid mouth!" Even while I was yelling, I knew I was making a major mistake. But I hated him so much! My mind flooded with the thousand insults, the blows, the abuse he'd poured on me since the first day I knew him.

Woody hit my shoulder—hard!—with his open hand and I stumbled backward.

"You're hurting me!" I yelled.

Instantly, Woody shot forward and shoved me again. *"Don't"*—shove— *"you"*—shove— *"call"*—shove— *"me"* —shove— *"stupid!"*

With the last shove, I staggered backward hard into a metal file cabinet and my head smashed into a sharp corner. For a moment I nearly went blind with pain.

I couldn't breathe. My knees gave way and I sank to the floor, barely aware of what was happening around me. The room erupted with voices. Greg was yelling something, and the next thing I knew, he was lying on the floor beside me. Woody kicked him in the ribs and then scrambled out of the room.

I tried to sit up, but my head was pounding. I knew I was crying, and I was furious with myself for my weakness. I heard laughter and Jennifer's voice saying, "Cute, Bridget. That was really cute."

"Leave her alone!" Mitzie shouted.

I heard Jennifer squeak, as if she'd been hurt. Mitzie helped me to my feet. "Are you all right?"

"She pinched me!" Jennifer squalled. "Mrs. Munson, Mitzie pinched me! Look at my arm!"

Sam pulled Greg to his feet. Greg's face was white and he pressed one hand against his side.

Mrs. Munson pushed Mitzie away from me. "You started this, Bridget. Go to Mr. Ziegler's office right now."

"She doesn't need the guidance counselor," Mitzie cried. "She needs the nurse."

"One more word and you're going to Mr. Ziegler's office, too," Mrs. Munson yelled.

"I'll be okay," I told Mitzie.

My head hurt, I was humiliated, and I was crying so hard I could barely see. I started for the door, one hand touching the wall for balance.

Behind me, Sam said to someone, "Greg needs help."

I stopped, but Mitzie was beside me again, pushing me gently toward the door. "Come on," she whispered. "We'll go to the nurse instead."

"Mitzie, sit down!" Mrs. Munson shouted.

"Go on," I told my friend. "I can make it."

I wavered down the hall toward Mr. Ziegler's office, only because it was much closer than the nurse's. He'd do something about Woody this time. He had to.

The final bell for first period rang, clanging in my head. I pressed my hands over my ears. I couldn't stand this, I couldn't stand this any more.

61

The front doors were between me and the guidance office. I stumbled toward them and left the building.

I wanted to go home, but that was too far to walk. The garden store was closer, but Dad . . . He wouldn't do anything. I wanted him to stand up for me, call the school, demand that Woody be expelled, that Mrs. Munson be fired. But he wouldn't do anything. He had never intervened between me and the bogeymen in my life. My bus had no driver, and now I didn't think my father was on it with me. His lack of courage humiliated me even more.

I went to Cait's house, doing my best to look and act as if nothing was wrong, but I stumbled over every curb and staggered against a high fence once. Finally I gave up trying to pretend that I was all right, and I held my aching head and cried. When I reached my aunt's front door, I knocked, but there was no answer.

I collapsed on the porch bench and tried to think. Under my fingers, the back of my head felt swollen where I'd hit it on the file cabinet. Swollen and wet. I looked at my fingers and saw blood.

I got back to my feet and walked around the house. There was a statue of Saint Francis in the flower bed by Cait's back door. She kept a spare key taped under the saint's outstretched hand. I used it to open the back door and stumbled into her kitchen.

The cats stared and followed me to the living room.

My head throbbed with each step. I dropped my backpack and let myself down gingerly onto the sofa.

Both cats jumped up beside me, still staring.

"Help me," I whispered.

I saw them touch faces, and a silvery dust glimmered in the air around them. The dust settled over my face and I fell asleep.

I woke when Cait came home. I sat up, and my head didn't hurt anymore, but the back of it was still swollen and sticky with blood.

The cats rushed at her, purring and meowing.

"I know, I know," she said, hurrying past them to kneel beside me. "Are you feeling better? I tried to help you as soon as Floss and Jasper let me know, but Bridget, this is what I was talking about! You must be willing to help yourself!"

"It was Woody," I began.

"I know," she said. She touched the back of my head gently with one hand while she traced a circle on my forehead with the other.

"I hate Woody! I wish—"

"Stop that," Cait said quietly, firmly. "Don't wish for anything when you're angry. You need a clear head before you wish, and you must never forget that you'll pay for it in kind. You might hurt him—you might even destroy him—but you would pay an exact price. And then you could involve all of us and put us in danger."

"I don't know what you mean," I said. "What are you talking about?"

She sighed. "Bridget, I know your head hurts, but try to concentrate on what I'm saying. You can protect yourself. You don't need to harm anyone. If you do, the price might be so great that we others will have to pay for you because you don't have resources yet, and you don't want that kind of debt."

I stared at her. "What others? What are you talking about?"

She cupped my face in her hands. "You must grow up now, Bridget. You must accept what you are."

I pushed her hands away. "What others? What did you mean?"

She shook her head and stood up. "I can't tell you anything until I see the signs I've been looking for. Show me that you accept the powers you inherited. Show me that you can and will take care of yourself without harming anyone. I can't tell you anything as long as you allow a stupid bully to injure you when you could have stopped him so easily."

"How?" I cried. "How?"

"Come into the bathroom," she said. "You need a shower so you can wash the blood out of your hair. The bleeding's stopped, but it's obvious that you've been in-jured. Your parents are going to be upset."

"They won't care," I said. "They'll tell me I should try to get along with Woody."

"And do you want to hear that again? How many times do you want to hope for help you know you'll never get? How many times before you learn to accept who you are?"

I glanced at my watch. Less than an hour had passed since I'd entered Mrs. Munson's room.

"I'll take a shower now but I won't go back to school," I said. "Not today. Can I wait here until the time I'd be going home? Mom's in Seattle."

She nodded. "I'll have to leave you for a while, but I want you to use the time to think about what I said. The cats will help you."

The cats, side by side at her feet, smiled.

"They're familiars, aren't they?" I blurted.

"Bridget, you exasperate me so! Of course they're fa-miliars!"

I held up one hand in protest. "Don't," I whispered. "Please don't tell me anything else."

For so long I had worked hard to push my powers down. Sometimes the effort wore me out. Now I was hurt, vulnerable. Scared. I must not let myself be tempted.

*   *   *

After I showered and washed my hair, Cait brewed a pot of tea, using herbs that would calm me, she said. She made me comfortable on her bed and put the tea and my favorite bone china cup on the table. The cats sat next to me, watching her.

"Take care of her," she told them before she left.

I drank a cup of tea and leaned back on the heap of pillows. One of the cats sat beside my head and the other sat by my feet.

Xiii appeared as a white parrot, squawking from the foot of the bed.

"You are not welcome," the cats told him in unison.

He disappeared, leaving a white feather on the bed.

"Barbarian," one of the cats whispered.

"Thug," the other whispered.

They smiled at me and said, "Sleep now while we show you what you most want to see."

I slept. When I awoke I couldn't remember what the cats had showed me, but I was smiling.

I felt completely well when I got to my feet. When I looked at my watch, I saw that I'd need to hurry if I wanted to catch Mitzie on the road home. I wanted to know what had happened after I left. The cats watched while I picked up my backpack and went to the door.

"Thanks," I said, feeling awkward and foolish. What would my friends think if they heard me? What would they think if they knew what happened here?

They wouldn't. I'd make sure of that.

Mitzie was barely half a block ahead of me when I reached the corner. I called to her to wait.

"What happened to you?" she asked. "Are you okay? You didn't come back to Munson's room, and when you didn't show up in trig, I was scared. I tried calling your house twice but no one answered. Julie and I didn't know what to do."

"I didn't go to the guidance office," I said. "I felt awful so I went to Cait's house and had a nap. It was closer than home."

"Oh, well, Cait's house," Mitzie said, sounding relieved. "Anybody would feel better going there instead of the guidance office."

"How was Greg?" I asked. "I was afraid he might have been badly hurt."

"Sam took Greg out of Munson's room while she was yelling at him to stop," Mitzie said. She grinned, then sobered again. "He called Greg's mom, and she drove right over to the school to take him to the doctor. Julie said she saw both Greg's parents going into the office after lunch. I hope Woody's really in trouble this time."

I hoped so, too, but the school had never done anything about him before, and he'd been hurting people since he first showed up for ninth grade. Why would they do something now?

Oh, Greg, I thought miserably. This is all my fault.

After we reached Mitzie's, I hurried a little, hoping to see Jordan and Althea. Jordan was nowhere in sight, but Althea was only a couple of blocks ahead. I ran to catch up.

"Are you all right?" she asked. "I worried about you. I'm sorry that you were hurt trying to help me."

"Thanks, but I'm fine now," I said. I saw her brown pocketbook under her arm. "Did you get your things back?"

She began to speak, hesitated, and then said, "I didn't have anything in it."

"Nothing?" I asked, trying not to stare.

She didn't respond. We were close to my house, so I said, "Why don't you come in for a while? We can have something to eat and maybe talk."

She shook her head. "I must go home," she said. "I'm glad you're all right. Thank you for helping me. I won't forget."

Then she walked swiftly away, her weird skirt and her strange, striped hair fluttering. She was heading for the fork in the road.

I watched her for a moment, and then, distracted by Bingo's howling, I hurried to let him out. He didn't waste much time but ran back inside a moment later. Xiii wasn't around, which surprised me. I expected him to have lots to say about what had happened at Cait's.

The neighborhood was quiet. There hadn't been time

for Althea to reach her home. I could follow her and see if she really lived in the house we had thought was condemned. If I was careful, she wouldn't know.

She said her pocketbook was empty. Why did she carry it, then? And why did she wear the same clothes every day?

I tossed my backpack inside the door and shut it. Bingo barked once.

I ran to the fork in the road and turned up the narrow twisting road to the cliff. Halfway there, as I rounded the sharpest curve, Althea stepped out of the woods in front of me.

"What do you want?" she asked in her husky voice.

For a moment I was too surprised to speak. Then I stammered, "I was worried about you. The cliff is dangerous. The house there was supposed to stay empty."

Althea's round dark eyes studied me. I struggled to keep my mind blank so she couldn't read it.

"The house is quite safe," she said calmly.

I couldn't think of anything else to say. I felt like an idiot. A nosy idiot.

"Wait right here and I'll see if my parents would like company," Althea said.

I nodded and watched her walk away. Why couldn't I wait a little closer? I couldn't even see the house from there.

I waited. And waited. I heard the dry flutter of wings

and looked up to see two falcons flying west. A light wind stirred the trees, and in the distance I heard a door close.

Althea appeared ahead of me. "It's all right," she called out. When I caught up with her, she said, "My parents want to meet you."

For a moment I was frightened, but then my curiosity took over. I followed her to the house and through the wide front door.

The house smelled of dust, and dust covered the bare wood floors. Althea led the way down a long hall into the large living room, but I stopped in the doorway. The room had a glass wall that overlooked Puget Sound. There was very little furniture, and what there was seemed to huddle in the darkest corner. Two small people stood in the shadows near it.

"Mother, Father, this is Bridget, the girl I told you about," Althea said. "Bridget, let me present my parents."

She was so formal, like a character out of a book.

I took two steps closer to the Peales. "How do you do?" I said.

Mr. Peale was shorter than his wife, but he didn't step forward into the light, so I couldn't see him clearly. Mrs. Peale answered for them both, saying, "We're glad to meet Althea's friend." Her voice was hoarse, like Althea's.

They dressed in gray and tan, their clothes almost indistinguishable in the poor light, and their hair was dark and without luster. I couldn't make out their features.

"Bridget worried that our house might not be safe," Althea said.

"Our house is quite safe," Mrs. Peale said. "But thank you for your concern, Bridget."

I felt awkward and embarrassed. The room seemed to grow larger in my imagination, and the Peales were even farther away. I didn't know what to say.

"I'll walk to the door with you," Althea said.

I turned toward the hall with relief. What a stupid idea, following her! I was afraid she thought I was an idiot.

"I'll see you tomorrow," I said.

"I'm glad you weren't hurt when you tried to help me," she said.

She closed the big door.

I ran all the way home.

Xiii sat under the moss rose. "Interesting people, aren't they?" he said when I approached him.

"What do *you* know about them?" I asked.

"Wouldn't you like to know?" he said.

I gritted my teeth. "If I kiss you, will you turn into a prince?"

"Try it," he said.

"Ugh," I said. "Not in a million years."

Xiii laughed. "Coward," he said. "Crybaby."

I slammed the front door and discovered that my headache had come back.

*　*　*

71

As soon as I got inside, I called Greg's house. His mother answered, and when I asked about Greg, she said he was asleep. "He has a cracked rib," she said. "This time Woody went too far. We complained, but the school won't do anything meaningful. All we got was a long story about his emotional problems, as if we cared. Are you all right, Bridget? What do your parents say?"

"I haven't had a chance to tell them anything yet," I said. I didn't want to think about that particular problem.

On my way to feed the quail, I knocked on Jordan's door, but no one answered. His father's truck still wasn't in the driveway. Xiii was probably right. He wasn't coming back. Did Jordan understand that?

I fed the quail alone, but on the way back, I knocked on the door again. Still no answer.

At home, xiii hung upside down from the branch of the maple tree. He had braided spider webs into his long red hair. A spider was still in one of the webs. I had a horrid hunch that the poor terrified thing would be a snack for later.

"You look ridiculous," I told him as I passed.

"Your mother's only three miles away and driving over the speed limit again," he retaliated. "You'd better think fast."

I hesitated and pressed one hand against my aching head.

Xiii laughed. "Don't blame me for the headache. I told you that trouble was coming. Maybe next time you'll listen. Think of how different things would have been if you had cast a circle around yourself and your new friend."

"You were eavesdropping on me and Cait," I accused. Xiii shrugged.

"The cats were right. You *are* a barbarian," I said.

He showed his small pointed teeth. "Cats!" he hissed.

I laughed.

He changed to the white parrot and flew screeching into the maple tree. The tree spirits protested, squeaking and chirping like disturbed sparrows.

"Bridget, Bridget!" they cried.

"Get back down here!" I called to xiii.

He appeared at my feet, a frog again. "More trouble's coming," he said. "Remember what I said."

He sounded almost happy about it, and he was supposed to be *my* threshold guardian!

chapter six

I checked the answering machine as soon as I got into the house. The single message was from one of Dad's old friends. No one from school had called about my cutting classes.

I took a deep breath and realized that my heart had been beating hard and fast. For a moment, I seriously considered doing my best to forget what had happened, because I couldn't be certain how Mom would react. She might be entirely sympathetic, but she might blame me for involving myself in something that wasn't any of my business.

I certainly wouldn't tell her I'd gone to Cait's. I knew better than that.

Dutifully I read the note Mom had left for me on the mantel, and I took the meat she wanted to cook out of the freezer. Bingo watched, thumping his tail on the floor and doing his best to smile.

"Later," I told him. "I'll sneak you some of the leftovers."

I was halfway through fixing a salad when the phone rang, and it startled me so much that I jumped.

It was Julie, calling to see if I was all right. While I assured her that I was, I ran my fingers under my hair, feeling for the scabs.

"We thought you were practically knocked out for a minute," she said. "I think even Jennifer was scared about how far Woody went, especially when you didn't show up for the rest of the day."

"I went to my aunt's," I said. "I wasn't in the mood to see Woody again."

"Oh, he didn't come back to school," Julie said. "But he cuts classes all the time, so that was no big surprise. What a rotten creep. Somebody ought to do something about him."

"Like what?" I asked bitterly. "I talked to Greg's mother. She said that when she complained to the school about Woody, all anybody would talk about were Woody's emotional problems."

"What about the emotional problems he's causing everybody else?" Julie said.

Suddenly I began laughing. "Do you know how ridiculous this sounds? Woody's been hurting people his whole life, and everybody who could help the rest of us is worrying about his 'emotional problems.'"

"You should have seen how he was treating Althea before you and Mitzie got to class. He sneaked around behind her and yanked her hair so hard I thought he'd break her neck. But listen, Bridget. She turned around and stared at him for a long time—she has the strangest eyes!—and nobody said a word, and Woody sort of backed up for a second. But then he grabbed her pocketbook—it was sitting on her desk—and started tossing it around, and you know how some of the boys are. They laughed and went along with it. Greg and Sam tried to stop them. . . ."

"What was Mrs. Munson doing?" I asked.

Julie snorted. "Sitting there and ignoring everything. Sometimes I wonder if she actually *likes* what Woody does. I know that sounds stupid, but it's almost as if he pulls off stuff that she'd like to do but doesn't dare."

Mom came in then, shedding her coat impatiently.

"I've got to go, Julie," I said. "See you tomorrow."

"What's new, Bridget?" Mom asked. She didn't wait for me to answer. "Traffic was awful, as usual." She put the meat into the microwave to defrost and filled a glass with water.

"Something happened at school this morning," I said after a moment.

Mom had been sipping her water, but she stopped. "Am I going to hate this?"

"I guess so," I said. "Woody McCready and his friends were picking on Althea, and when I tried to help, he shoved me into a file cabinet and then hurt Greg when he tried to stop him. Mrs. Munson sent me to the guidance counselor, but I left school instead because my head hurt so much. It was bleeding." I touched my head gingerly.

"Did you call your father? Why didn't you call me? Let me see it."

Mom parted my hair and I heard her suck in her breath. "It's scabbed over already, but you'd better be careful when you brush your hair. Does your head still ache?"

"Not too much," I said.

"Maybe I should take you to the doctor," she said uncertainly.

"No, no. I don't need to see him. But Mrs. Thompson took Greg to the emergency room. He's got a cracked rib where Woody kicked him."

Mom sighed. "Greg shouldn't have been fighting him."

"He wasn't!" I exclaimed. "He was trying to get him away from me, and Woody knocked him down and then kicked him."

"Oh, Bridget," Mom said, sighing again. "Why do you get involved with things that aren't any of your business?

I'm sure Althea could have taken care of herself. If you just ignored Woody, he'd leave you alone, but you do things that goad him. He hit you last year and it was because you were interfering then, too."

"He was throwing lighted matches at Mitzie!"

"It's not as if he set her on fire, Bridget," she said, exasperated. "Some boys act like that. You have to learn to ignore them."

Hopeless. It was always hopeless.

I shredded carrots for the salad and blinked hard enough to keep tears out of my eyes. I could feel Mom's mind buzzing and buzzing while it tested everything I'd said, looking for another line of attack, desperate to shape me up, keep me on a shelf where I couldn't do any harm or start anything or bring unknown devils home or crash down the roof. Or . . . or . . . The shredder nicked my thumb and blood oozed slowly.

Mom tested the meat in the microwave and, satisfied, took it out. Bingo, who had left the kitchen the first time Mom sighed, crept back in and looked up at me.

"Do you want out?" I asked as I sucked the blood off my thumb and wished my skin was still whole.

Bingo ran to the back door and I followed to open it for him. He dashed out, jumped over xiii, and ran down the deck steps.

Xiii hopped close to me. "What a fuss," he said. "You could end all of it. You'd know the ways, if you'd just look where you're supposed to look and listen when you're supposed to listen. The cut on your thumb—it wasn't even there, and yet you were ready to start whining over it! Look! Look at your thumb, you brat, and see what you can do when you try!"

I looked. There was no cut.

"See?" he cried triumphantly. "See what you can do when you *act with knowledge about the real world* instead of debating everything ugly in the one you think you live in?"

I went back inside, my heart thumping again. I didn't know what he was talking about, I told myself firmly. I'd wished automatically, quickly, without even thinking. Didn't everyone at a time like that?

Or had I become different once more? Did my wishes click into reality now the way they had when I was a child? Would I have to push down the powers I didn't want the way I'd had to before, in order to be accepted?

Mom wasn't done talking yet. "Take my advice, Bridget. Try listening to me for once in your life. You're stuck with Woody, so make up your mind to ignore him."

My mother's advice was useless. It was actually cruel. In her world, in the world I actually wanted to be a part of, Woody couldn't be ignored.

Maybe xiii was right. In his world, Woody was a bad dream, not a true dream. I could drift there and stay and then Mom's world, Woody's world, would only be a mean kind of fantasy. But then I'd be what Cait was, and I'd be *known*. Known the way Cait was known. People sensed what she was. Some of them hated her for it without even knowing the good she could do. And *would* do, if only they let her. Lots of people gossiped about her. A few people crossed the street to avoid her. Did I want that for the rest of my life when things were already so hard for me? When some kids knew that I was different, even though I pushed away the few powers I had?

"Don't sulk, Bridget," Mom said. "I can always tell when you're sulking."

I opened my mouth to protest and then shut it again.

When Dad came home, Mom explained her version of how I'd been hurt, but I didn't argue. Dad sighed and said, "Oh, Bridget." But in his mind, he said, "Oh, chickie."

I gritted my teeth hard. I didn't want to know my parents' thoughts.

During dinner, Dad said, "I haven't seen O'Neal's truck in his driveway for several days. Has Jordan said anything about his father going out of town?"

"No. But I haven't had a chance to talk to Jordan for a couple of days. He hasn't been showing up when I feed the quail."

"Did you knock on their door?" Mom asked. "I don't want you knocking on their door and involving yourself in whatever's going on." In her mind, she saw me kissing Jordan in the hall inside the O'Neals' front door. I slammed my mental door shut, fast.

"No, I didn't knock," I lied angrily.

"Well, don't," Mom said. Scowling, she sliced through her steak.

Keep your mouth shut, xiii warned me from somewhere.

I took his advice.

As soon as I finished eating, I called Greg again and was surprised when he answered the phone himself.

"How are you?" I asked.

"How are *you?*" he countered. "Mom said you sounded okay when you called earlier, but I don't see how you could be. I thought Woody had almost knocked you out."

How much could I tell him? "My head hurt, so I left school and went to Cait's and had a nap."

"I bet that's not all that happened," he said. "What did she do? Give you tea made of scorpion tails and bat toenails?"

"Not funny," I said. "Are you going to school tomorrow?"

"Wouldn't miss it," Greg said cheerfully.

"Don't try to help me again if Woody starts something with me," I said. "I can handle it myself."

Greg laughed, said, "Ouch!" and then said, "Laughing

hurts my rib. Yeah, I saw how you handle things yourself."

"I mean it, Greg. I can take care of myself."

There was a long pause, and then Greg said, "How long did you stay at Cait's?" He sounded a little amused. Just a little, as if he already knew.

"See you tomorrow," I said, and I hung up.

The phone rang immediately. When I answered, Cait asked, "Did everything go all right?"

I knew what she meant. "No big deal," I said.

I wanted to talk to her, but I didn't dare.

Cait understood. "I'll talk to you some other time," she said.

Later, in my room, I took out my watercolor and studied it for a long time. What bird should go in the space I'd left? A hawk? A falcon? I wanted one or the other, but I couldn't decide. I paged through my bird books, looking at pictures. Cait had offered snapshots to me, but I hadn't taken them.

I didn't have much time left before I'd have to turn in the watercolor for the art fair, but there was nothing in me that night that could create anything beautiful. I put the painting away and opened my bedroom window.

Xiii hung from a tree branch close by, combing his

long hair with what looked like the dried foot of a tiny creature. He was hard to bear sometimes.

No, he was often hard to bear.

"You're no walk in the park yourself, chickie," he said. He dropped the foot and swung closer to the window. "Jordan's home. His father left a little money, but that's nearly gone. Jordan's looking for work here and there. He asked your father for a job, but this is the wrong season for extra help at the store."

"Dad didn't say anything about that," I protested.

"Well, he wouldn't, would he?" xiii said.

"What should Jordan do?" I asked.

"You tell me," xiii said.

Anger seared me. "What good are you?" I cried.

Bingo, who had been tolerating the conversation so far, ran out of my bedroom.

Xiii snickered. "If it's any comfort to you, that stupid dog will live to be nineteen years old and die in his sleep after a full meal of doggie stew and a chocolate chip cookie. Years from now you'll get another dog just like him and your granddaughter Lael will play with him in your studio. She told me so."

I stared. "My granddaughter? My *granddaughter*? Are you crazy?"

"No, but she sometimes wonders about you," xiii said. "Oh yes, she's here sometimes, waiting and hoping you'll pull up your socks." He made that grunting sound I hated so much and turned into an owl, then flew soundlessly away.

My headache was worse.

At school the next morning, Woody and I were called out of first period to the guidance counselor's office. He smirked and I seethed. While we waited side by side on hard plastic chairs, he muttered constantly under his breath, not to me but to himself, apparently rehearsing what he was going to say. "She hurt me, no, they hurt me, no, they kicked me so hard I needed to go to the emergency room. . . ."

I was called in first. Mr. Ziegler, who had combed six dark hairs over the top of his bald head, read to me from a sheet of paper. "Physical attack in class, left school without permission. . . ."

"Here's my note," I said, and I passed him the note Mom had written for me that morning.

He opened the envelope without looking at me even once, read what Mom had written, and nodded his head.

"Your mother says that after you were injured, you went home to rest," he said as if he had found Mom's note impossible to believe.

I sat there, waiting, watching the scramble going on in his mind as if it was a bad cartoon show. He wanted coffee, he was hungry, he hated Woody and knew that he was waiting outside, he wondered if Woody carried a knife, and his right shoe hurt his foot.

"Sorry," I said.

"Thanks," he said. "It's been getting worse. I think it's the weather."

He folded Mom's note and put it back in the envelope, hoping that the gesture would somehow bring everything to a close but knowing it wouldn't.

"You don't get along with Woody very well, do you?" he said in despair.

"No one does," I said.

"Yes," he said. "Well, try to get along with Mrs. Munson." He shuffled a mess of papers on his desk. "I hope you're feeling better today."

"Not really," I said.

"Fine," he said. "You may go now."

As I left, I tried to prop up his courage with all the mental strength I could gather together, but I saw Woody still muttering in his chair, and I knew there was nothing I could do to help Mr. Ziegler. His foot hurt too much. His bad dream was too real.

When I returned to class, Mrs. Munson gave me her best die-where-you-stand look, I smiled, and then I took my seat. Althea, dressed as always in her strange tan clothes, nodded her head. I nodded back.

"What did Ziegler say?" Mitzie hissed at me.

"Mitzie, can't you keep quiet for one minute?" Mrs. Munson asked.

The bell rang, saving us and sending us to trig.

Jordan was in our art class that afternoon, and I stopped beside him. "How've you been?" I asked.

"Fine."

"I miss you when I'm feeding the quail," I said as I wondered if I'd lost my mind completely. "One of them was limping this morning, and he seemed to be missing some of his feathers."

"I'll have a look this afternoon," he said. "I'll bring some of the cracked corn."

Althea, next to him, smiled at me and then looked out the window.

Remembering Jordan's promise, I smiled much too much for the rest of the class.

But he didn't come out of his house when I crossed through his yard to feed the quail. Rain began falling when I was in the woods, and that fit my new mood completely.

Rain fell steadily for the rest of the week. Mitzie caught a cold and stayed home for two days, so I walked to and from school alone. I never saw Althea on the road in the mornings, and in the afternoons she hurried ahead of me so fast that she was out of sight almost immediately. She wore an old brown raincoat that helped her blend into the brush, and I wondered if she'd chosen the color deliberately.

She still sat at our cafeteria table every day, silent and watchful. The other girls gave up trying to involve her in conversation, but it didn't seem to bother her. Nothing bothered her. Her round dark eyes observed everything but gave nothing back. Not even to me.

I fed the quail alone, morning and afternoon, all week. And in spite of my mother's warning, I knocked on Jordan's door again on Friday afternoon.

After a long time, he answered.

"Bridget," he said. He looked tired and not very happy to see me. His mind was clouded with worry and hurt.

"I guess your dad didn't come back," I said. "Have you heard from him?"

"Sure," he said, lying. It didn't take a witch to see that.

I blinked and waited for a moment. Then I said, "Do you need something? Is there anything I can do for you?"

He shook his head.

"Want to walk back to feed the quail with me?" I asked. "You haven't seen them for a while."

"I've got a lot of homework," he said. "Maybe tomorrow."

He closed the door gently, carefully, so he wouldn't hurt my feelings. I felt the pang that he felt. It ran through me like an electric shock and nearly stopped my breath.

When I got home, I found that xiii had taken shelter under a fallen maple leaf. His green skin glistened. He was playing with a dead beetle, and when he saw me watching him, he pushed it toward me.

"How about a snack before dinner?" he said.

"I could step on you and squash you flat," I said.

He grunted and nearly exploded into his dragon form. He bent his head over me and hissed.

"You don't scare me," I said.

"Liar," he said.

"Creep," I answered.

"Coward," he snapped back.

"Stop it, stop it!" a dozen tree spirits cried from deep within the cedar tree.

"Trouble's coming," xiii said, and he sounded pleased.

"Trouble's already been here!" I shouted. "Didn't you notice?"

"Are you talking about what happened with Woody yesterday?" xiii asked slyly. "That wasn't real trouble. No, that was only a wart. A sneeze. A cow pie."

"Not to me, it wasn't," I said.

He snapped audibly into his boy-shape. "Bridget, listen. You need all your powers for what's coming."

"It's close, Bridget, close," the tree spirits cried.

I hurried inside.

chapter seven

That night I had a dream that seemed so real, so beauti-ful—and so terrible—that I knew I would remember it for the rest of my life.

I dreamed I rode on a white horse that waded in a shal-low, rocky stream. Spring sunlight warmed us and a thou-sand strange birds sang in the forest. I knew I was going to my own home, not my parents' home. The horse didn't need my guidance but left the water for a narrow mossy path that wound into the trees. A large gray bird with round black eyes flew to my shoulder and clung there. The air was scented with wild plum blossoms and ferns.

We reached a clearing and I saw a low house made of glass and wood. The horse stopped to let me slide off her back.

Suddenly a stranger appeared in the open doorway,

someone made of shouts and shadows and acrid smoke. The bird fell dead at my feet. The horse reared and ran away.

"Oh, please, no . . ." I began.

I woke, crying for the loss of the house that I knew was mine and for the death of the bird who had made the mistake of trusting me. I pulled my blankets over my head, as if that childish gesture could protect me from what was coming.

Bingo huddled close to me and whined.

On Saturday morning, I walked through a light drizzle to the garden store. Dad had told me at breakfast that Greg's injuries would keep him from working for several days.

"Why don't you hire Jordan to replace him?" I'd asked.

Dad had made a gesture, opened his mouth, then shut it again. Finally he'd said, "I wouldn't want him to get the idea I could keep him on all winter. I'll barely have enough work for Greg when he comes back."

I didn't need to ask who would be doing Greg's work until then. To fortify myself, I ate two more pieces of bacon.

I restocked shelves until my arms ached. Mitzie, still coughing, came in for a quick visit and left to meet Julie at the mall. Greg showed up next, to apologize because I was doing all the heavy work, and then he asked me if I wanted to go to a movie with him sometime.

I gawked at him. He'd never asked me out, and neither had anyone else. Like Mitzie and Julie, I'd decided that I'd probably never have an official date.

Greg misunderstood my silence. "Hey, it was just an idea," he said as he shuffled his feet. "I thought that maybe . . ." He stopped and looked miserable, as if he was expecting me to sock him.

What would Jennifer Budd do at a moment like this?

I cleared my throat. "Maybe we *could* go to a movie," I said finally.

He grinned but he looked embarrassed. He might have said more, but Cait came into the store then, and Greg abandoned me for her. He actually seemed relieved.

When he walked out the door a few minutes later, Cait put a green gardener's jacket over her orange embroidered tunic and helped me load the last of the bags of grass seed on the shelves.

"Greg seemed happy," she said.

"He asked me to go to a movie with him sometime," I said. I stopped to catch my breath and push my hair out of my eyes.

"He's a sweetie," she said. She didn't bother hiding her smile. "He won't break your heart."

"Hey!" I said. "Don't get any ideas."

"Of course not. I'm the last one to encourage you to

get serious about a boy. How's your watercolor coming along? Have you finished it yet?"

I stacked small boxes of grass seed on a middle shelf while I said, "I can't decide if I want to put a hawk on the fence or a falcon. Maybe I should have borrowed your snapshots. None of the pictures in my bird books are very exciting."

"Go to the place you've painted and hang around for a while," she said as she brushed dust off her jacket. "Maybe a bird will land on the fence and make your decision for you. But don't consciously call one. This is a good chance for you to see what happens when you don't do anything but live in the present moment."

I pulled a case of slug bait off the cart and cut it open with my pocket knife. "I walk past that fence all the time, but I never see a bird on it anymore."

"That's the trouble," Cait said. "You walk past."

We worked in silence for a few minutes, and then she said, "How's school been going?" She probably knew, but she wanted to hear my version of events.

"Are you asking if Woody has done anything else to me? No. He cuts first period most of the time, and I don't have any other classes with him."

"But when he's in class?" Cait asked. "Then what?"

"I don't make eye contact with him. He stays busy making Sam miserable, but he'll get back to me sooner or later." I straightened the shelf of slug bait boxes and wondered if Woody would melt if someone poured the bait on him.

"It doesn't have to be that way," Cait said. "And you shouldn't spend your energy thinking about revenge, even if you're only joking." She touched a box with one finger, pushing it slightly out of line.

Before I had a chance to respond and defend my thoughts, she turned away to help a customer.

She thinks it's so easy to accept the powers, I thought, and I was almost resentful of her.

Maybe it really was easy. Maybe, if I accepted what went with the powers and quit worrying, I'd find that it was easy to open all the doors I'd been shutting since kindergarten. I was different from the other kids anyway, and they already knew it.

No, no. Just thinking about it caused my stomach to tie into a knot. I knew what the other kids called me behind my back—*weird, spooky, strange, crazy.* Add those to *clumsy* and *dork,* and it wasn't hard to understand why I never expected to be invited to the parties Jennifer and her friends gave. How much worse could it get if I accepted the powers I'd been born with and used them?

A staple had come out of one of the boxes and lay on the shelf directly in front of me. I raised my hand over it and called to it in my mind, and it flew up to my palm. I lifted my hand away from it and it hung in the air, turning slowly.

"Stop it!" hissed Cait.

The staple fell to the floor and my face burned. I felt ridiculous.

"What was *that* all about?" she demanded.

"I just wanted to see if I could still pick up metal things, needles and paper clips—"

"It's childish," Cait said. She looked around to see if anyone was near enough to hear us. "Bridget! Listen to me! Make up your mind to either accept the craft or reject it totally, but don't insult yourself and all of us with silly tricks."

I looked up at her. "Who is 'all of us'? You mention other people, but you never tell me who they are."

"You aren't ready for that," she said. "Not if you're picking up trash in your father's store with anything but your fingers. We don't use our powers to impress people, or to entertain others or to make money—and by the way, we certainly don't use them to frighten people or to get even. You know that."

Dad appeared suddenly from the next aisle. "Is there a problem, Cait? Bridget?"

"No problem," Cait said briskly. "We're done here. I think I'll take a turn at the cash register."

She walked away from me, and in my mind, I heard a great stone door swing shut.

Tears spurted into my eyes.

"What's wrong, chickie?" Dad asked. "Not up to working today?"

"I'm okay, Dad. I know you need my help."

He touched my shoulder sympathetically. "You've had a bad week. Take off early today. Maybe you and Mitzie can do something together."

"Sure," I said. I turned back to the boxes on the cart and cut open another. Dad shuffled off, sighing. He was almost as good at it as Mom.

Before I left, Cait hugged me and apologized. "I get so impatient, waiting for you," she said. "I know better. I know you have to consent to your powers. But I love you so much. It hurts me to see you so miserable."

What is it like for you, I wondered. But all I said was, "See you later." When I left the store, I didn't look back.

I hurried along the road that led home. When I reached the fence I'd put in my watercolor, I was surprised to see a quail perched there. Usually they hid in the middle of the afternoon. As I drew closer, the quail crouched a little, preparing to fly away. I stopped. The quail hesitated but didn't trust me. She watched me first with one eye and then with the other. Her topknot quivered.

Suddenly she froze. At the same instant I heard wings overhead. When I looked up, I saw a falcon outlined against the gray sky. The quail was a perfect target, too far away from the trees to escape the falcon if it decided to stoop, to drop down at the almost unimaginable speed it would use when hunting.

"No!" I cried.

Instantly, the falcon soared away, as if it had understood.

The quail flapped noisily into the woods, crying its alarm, which was echoed immediately by a dozen other quail hidden in the trees.

I felt my pulse thud in my throat. That was too close. There were so few quail left that losing another would break my heart.

I was shaking when I walked toward home.

Xiii was waiting for me as usual, squatting in the middle of the path.

"Don't say anything," I said. "I'm having a bad witch day."

I passed him, went into the house, and headed straight for the kitchen with Bingo close behind. Suddenly I was starving.

Mom wasn't home, but I hadn't expected her to be there. She'd said at breakfast that she might go shopping. I made a sandwich for myself and another for Bingo, and we ate them in the living room in front of the TV, scattering crumbs around as if I wouldn't be the one who vacuumed them up. I was determined not to think about

what had happened at the store, but it was all I could concentrate on.

Exactly what powers did I have? Oh, yes, I could do
tricks. I had amused myself with them when I was a little
kid, but only when I was alone in my bedroom. I couldn't
even remember how young I'd been when I'd learned
that when my parents were in the room, I'd better not
move things around without touching them or turn lights
on and off.

I could read the minds of most people, if I wanted
to. There were a few people who closed their minds
to me successfully. Other people, ones like Woody
and Mrs. Munson and a neighbor we'd had in Seattle,
had such ugly minds that I couldn't bear to look into
them.

I knew what people would say before they said it.
When I let myself, I knew when the phone would ring.

I saw tree spirits all the time, and sometimes I saw the
different kinds of earth spirits, those tall, pale beings who
danced and sang by starlight. I heard water spirits call out
from lakes and ponds, telling the history of those places
so that anyone who could hear would remember and tell
the stories after the lakes and ponds were gone and the
earth became a desert.

I could speak to animals and birds, and I had done so,
until I was six years old. Even stones had told me their

stories. The winds had told me about everything that had ever been, long before I started school.

Once, when I'd passed through crowds, I'd known which people had the powers, who used them, and who didn't.

And, when I was being truthful with myself, I knew who hated me and why.

Woody. Jennifer. Their special friends. They hated me but they weren't certain why. I hated them and I knew why.

I lost my appetite and gave the rest of my sandwich to Bingo.

What if I completely forgot that I'd ever had powers? Would I be like everyone else then?

Or would I still have that "otherness" about me?

Later, when I went to the woods to feed the quail, Jordan ran after me.

"You're home!" I exclaimed when I saw him climb over the fence.

"Sure," he said. "Have you seen the falcons again? I saw them this morning."

"I saw one this afternoon," I said. "There was a quail on the fence down the road and a falcon overhead. For a moment, I was afraid the quail would be caught."

"We don't want to lose any more," he said.

"We," he'd said. We.

"No, we don't," I said. But it had been close. It needn't have happened at all if I'd thought to cast a circle.

We sat together on the stump and waited. After a few minutes, the quail came out and ate. The one who had limped before seemed better. I chose to take it as a good omen.

Was Jordan glad to be with me? I could have found out, but I was afraid of what I might discover in his mind.

Greg had asked me to go out with him. Jordan never had.

After the quail left, we walked out of the woods.

"See you tomorrow, maybe," Jordan said as he headed for his house.

"Jordan?" I called out.

He stopped and looked back.

"Have you heard from your dad?"

"Sure," he said. "He calls every couple of days. He's got a job and he'll come back as soon as he can."

That time I deliberately looked into his mind, and saw the despair and the late-night fear. He was lying.

I swallowed hard and said, "Good. I'm glad, Jordan."

I didn't wait to see him go inside his empty house.

chapter Eight

I woke Sunday morning determined to finish the watercolor. After breakfast, I walked up the road to see the fence again and decide, finally, what the bird would be.

A thin fog hung shimmering in the woods. A dozen tree spirits chattered and gossiped in a birch where the leaves hung golden and wet in the windless morning. An earth spirit wandered toward a clump of cedars, humming to herself and weaving yellowed grasses into her long silver hair.

"Good morning," I called out to all of them. "Good morning."

"Bridget, Bridget!" the tree spirits cried. "See, it's Bridget!"

The earth spirit looked back at me and raised one hand. She included my name in her song.

A peregrine falcon sat on the fence, her dark eyes calm. I stood absolutely still, hardly daring to breathe. She was beautiful.

"I'll paint you," I told her with certainty. "You're exactly right."

I focused my attention on her, trying to memorize every mark on every feather. I imagined how I would paint her, what colors I'd use.

She didn't move. I wondered what she thought of me, standing there and staring so hard at her.

Her eyes grew darker, larger. I couldn't stop looking at her. It seemed as if the world stopped. Something was about to happen.

Then in an instant, she blurred, faded, the air around her glimmered and hummed—and there sat Althea.

Was it really Althea?

"Who are you?" I cried.

Althea sat on the top rail, her chevron skirt tucked close to her legs, her gaze fixed on me.

I wasn't able to speak. She seemed to be in charge of the silence, in charge of everything. She expected me to accept what I'd just seen as if it were an ordinary occurrence, as if I saw birds change into people every day of my life.

She's a shape-shifter, I thought. I wrenched myself free from her gaze and began running up the road, tripping over my feet and almost in tears.

I heard wings and glanced back. The spell was broken. The falcon had taken flight.

I didn't stop running until I reached Mitzie's. I was breathless, so I waited near her garage while I got control of myself again. I didn't want what I had seen to be true.

It wouldn't *be* true if I could talk to Mitzie about ordinary things and put the shape-shifter out of my mind. School. Homework. Books. Clothes. Those plain and simple things would heal me of . . . what? My delusions?

No, I had seen true.

Who was Althea Peale? Why was she here?

When my hands stopped shaking, I ran up the steps to Mitzie's front door and rang the bell.

Anna answered, holding a jelly sandwich in one hand. She didn't speak to me, but instead yelled, "Mitzie!" at the top of her lungs and walked away.

Mitzie appeared immediately. "Hey," she said when she saw me. "I was going to call you in a few minutes. Did you finish your trig homework?"

I shook my head. "I haven't started it yet."

She looked at me strangely. "Are you okay? You look like you saw a ghost."

I almost laughed. "No, but if you offer me a sandwich like Anna's I won't turn it down."

"Oh, gosh, I'm sorry," Mitzie said. "Come in. We're having a snack before lunch. Mom and Dad drove into

Seattle, so we can eat anything we want while they're gone."

I followed Mitzie to the kitchen and sat on a stool while she made the sandwich. Anna poured milk into a glass for me, slopping a lot of it on the tile counter, but Mitzie didn't say anything.

"Have you seen Jordan?" Mitzie asked while we ate.

"He fed the quail with me last night. He said his dad calls him a lot and is coming home pretty soon." I felt guilty telling Mitzie something I knew wasn't true.

"I hope he does come home," Mitzie said. "Poor Jordan. I'd hate staying alone in a house."

"You're afraid of those creaky noises in the attic," Anna said. She had a ring of milk around her mouth and a dribble of it down the front of her T-shirt.

"*You're* afraid of the noise the refrigerator makes," Mitzie retorted.

"Jordan is weird," Anna said. "He doesn't have any friends."

"How would you know?" Mitzie demanded. She refilled my glass and poured more milk for herself.

"I see him walking down the road all the time by himself," Anna said. "He's the weirdest kid I ever saw except for Althea Peale."

"You know Althea?" I asked.

Anna nodded. "Sure. I hated her clothes. Everybody did. The kids in class made fun of her."

"What are you talking about?" Mitzie asked. "How do you know what the kids do?"

Anna stared at her. "Mitzie, she was in my class," she said with a great pretense of patience. "Why shouldn't I know what the kids did?"

"*Your* class?" I asked. "Anna, are you sure you know what you're talking about?"

Anna raised her chin. "I'm talking about skinny weird Althea Peale who has funny hair."

"But she goes to high school!" Mitzie protested.

"She's nine years old!" Anna yelled. "She didn't get double-promoted that much after she left Sunset Heights."

For a long moment, we stared at each other. "A girl named Althea Peale was in your class for a while?" I asked carefully.

Anna nodded, her mouth full.

"It's not a very common name," Mitzie said, musing.

"Do you know where she lived?" I asked, almost afraid to hear the answer.

Anna shook her head, swallowed, and said, "Nope. I never asked her and I didn't care. She was only there the first couple of weeks of school and then she left. I didn't like her because she was always watching everybody. You know, snooping and spying."

Mitzie shook her head. "You've got everything all mixed up."

Anna jumped up, spilling the last of her milk on the counter. "I don't have *anything* mixed up!" she said. "I don't want to talk to you anymore. I want to watch cartoons."

After she left the room, Mitzie groaned. "What a brat. She makes things up all the time and gets everybody else so confused that we don't know what *we're* talking about, either. I can hardly wait until she gets to high school and has Mrs. Munson for a class. Talk about sweet revenge, on both of them!"

I laughed a little with her—imagining how Mrs. Munson would deal with Anna would make anybody laugh—but I felt as if I'd just seen into someone else's nightmare.

Althea Peale went to grade school for the first two weeks of the school year?

And she was only nine years old?

The sandwich I was trying to eat tasted like ashes. I wanted to see Cait and talk to her about this. But at the same time, I was afraid to know what Cait would tell me.

And didn't I already know what she'd say?

Althea Peale was a shape-shifter. She was girl and falcon, and she could be any age she wanted. But why?

I stayed at Mitzie's longer than I should have, and when I left, a sudden soft rush of rain soaked my light jacket. I hurried until I saw the fence where Althea had been sitting, and then, unwillingly, I stopped.

She wasn't there. But I was frightened, so I broke into a run, as if I was fleeing for my life. I saw Jordan's house with its empty driveway, and my house, safe and ordinary.

No one in my house would believe in shape-shifters. As long as I was inside, I wouldn't have to believe either.

Xiii dangled upside down from a branch, swinging a little. When I started up the walk, he called out, "So. What did you think of the shape-shifter?"

I stopped reluctantly, hunching my shoulders against the rain. "Why is she here?"

"A better question would be 'What's going to happen to her?'"

I shook my head. "I don't understand."

"Trouble's coming," he said, mimicking his frog voice. "Did you forget so soon?"

"What's she going to do?" I asked. I shuddered suddenly. Had the day grown cold?

"She isn't going to do anything to hurt you or anybody else," xiii said. "Don't you find her to be unusually—umm—childlike? Or perhaps I should say—vulnerable?"

"You mean for a shape-shifter?" I asked, laughing bitterly. "I wouldn't know. She's the first one I ever met, unless I count you."

Xiii snickered. "The *first* one? That's what you think. And for your information, I am most definitely *not* a shape-shifter." His mood changed, and I could tell from his sour face that he was about to work himself up into a rage again. "Can't you tell the difference between what I am and a plain, ordinary shape-shifter? Do you take pleasure in being so stupid? I fail to see the satisfaction."

"Wait a minute," I said. I moved a little closer to him. "Are there other shape-shifters around?"

Xiii righted himself on the branch, scowled, and swung his legs. "I refuse to answer questions with obvious answers. If you want to know who's a shape-shifter, then just *look*. But none of that has anything to do with the falcon's problems. Trouble is coming, and it involves you and the skinny bird girl. The ones who want to crush the spirit out of you will crush her completely. She's weak, because she's not her true self. And neither are you."

And then, because he was impossible, he vanished completely, leaving me with a crick in my neck because I had looked up for so long.

When I went inside, I woke up both Dad and Bingo. They'd been dozing in front of the TV, although how they managed to sleep through the racket of a football game was beyond me. I stripped off my wet jacket and hung it on the closet doorknob.

"Where've you been?" Dad asked.

I told him I'd gone to Mitzie's. "I haven't finished my homework yet so I'd better get started," I said. I'd heard Mom banging pots in the kitchen, and I wanted to get to my room before she thought up something for me to do.

I hadn't vacuumed the carpet for days and didn't want to be stuck doing it. I wanted to work on my watercolor.

I ran upstairs and took it out of my portfolio. Did I really want to put the peregrine in the painting?

I sat down at my desk and looked blindly at the wall.

The peregrine was Althea. No, I couldn't put her in my painting. It would be a constant reminder of what I'd seen, and I didn't want to know about things like that.

Maybe I wouldn't even enter my watercolor in the art fair. Maybe I'd just forget the whole thing.

I got up and then sat down again.

Would Jennifer and her friends like me any better if I didn't enter my watercolor? Probably not. Would they stop ridiculing me? I doubted it.

Would Woody promise never to hit me again if I tore up my watercolor and threw it away? I shook my head. No.

I walked to the window and looked out. The rain had stopped. Matted wet leaves lay in heaps on the lawn. Spring was so far away, and I didn't know how I could bear the long winter ahead. Winter and the school I'd come to hate and the bus without a driver.

Stop thinking this way! I told myself. Just stop it!

I carried my water cup to the bathroom, filled it, and got out my paints. Then I carefully drew a peregrine falcon sitting on the fence.

I had just finished my watercolor when the time came

to feed the quail. I felt better about everything. When I ran across the street on my way to the woods, I stopped by Jordan's house and knocked on the door. I expected him to answer. I expected him to go with me.

After a long time he opened the door. He looked surprised. "Is it that time?" he asked.

"You must have been expecting me," I said. "You're wearing your jacket."

He blinked, then said, "Yeah, sure. Wait a sec while I get some cracked corn."

I waited and watched the watery afternoon sunshine glitter in the alder trees. There were no tree spirits hiding among the leaves. Probably there never had been. Maybe the only thing wrong with me was my vivid imagination. Jordan came out with the can of cracked corn, and we climbed the fence to the woods. The only sound we heard was water dripping from the trees.

"I saw three peregrine falcons today," Jordan said. "I was down on the beach, past the old dock, and I looked up and there they were, circling around the cliff where the big slide happened last spring."

I hugged myself to keep from shivering.

The quail crept out, ate, and went into hiding again. As we walked back to his house, Jordan asked me if I was entering something in the art fair.

"Yes, a four-seasons thing with birds," I said as I stumbled over a clump of ferns. He was interested in my art!

"Good," he said. "I hope you win."

But he didn't think I could. I didn't want to read his mind, but his thoughts were there, written in a book that was open to me. He thought that Greg would win again, and he was sorry for me.

And then he forgot about me even while we were climbing his fence together. He wondered about his father. He wondered how the man could call—even if he wanted to—because the phone service had been cut off.

I ran away from him without saying good-bye. I hated mind reading! What good was it?

When I reached my front walk, xiii was crouched directly in my path.

"I'll tell you what good it is," he said. "At least you get some warning when the sky is ready to fall."

I aimed a kick at him, but he leaped out of the way and laughed at me.

I slammed the front door so hard that I woke up my father and Bingo again.

chapter Nine

On Monday, I left for school earlier than usual because I wanted to turn in my watercolor to Miss Ireland before first period. I'd called Mitzie, so she was waiting on her porch. She wanted to see it, but I told her she'd have to wait until the art fair.

"You'll say you like it even if you don't," I said. "I'm already worried about what the judges will think."

"You're terrific," she said. "Don't worry."

I opened my mouth and shut it again. I'd nearly told her what Jordan thought.

"Hey," Mitzie said, looking back. "I see Althea. Do you want to wait for her?"

"No!" I blurted. Althea. She was just a girl! There was no such thing as a shape-shifter.

And there was no such thing as a threshold guardian, either. Xiii may have been sitting impudently on my gate that morning, but he wasn't real and I could safely ignore him.

"I thought you liked Althea," Mitzie said. She looked shocked.

I sighed. "I do, I do. But she'll probably want to know what's in the portfolio and I don't want to show her and then she'll think I'm rude and . . ."

"Okay!" Mitzie said. "I get the point, Bridget. Gosh, what's wrong with you?"

"Nothing," I said. "Nothing except I hate school and that's where we're going, and Mrs. Munson is probably hanging upside down from the rafters in the school basement and wondering what she can do to us today."

Mitzie sputtered laughter. "Maybe she sleeps in a coffin."

"No, that's Woody," I said.

Mitzie's smile disappeared. "Mom doesn't think he's got emotional problems. She says he's just plain rotten and does exactly what he likes and enjoys every minute of it, so why is everybody supposed to be sorry for him?"

"I like your mom," I said.

Mitzie wasn't a passenger on the bus with no driver.

Miss Ireland seemed pleased when I turned over my watercolor. "I'll show you the mat," she said as she started pulling open flat drawers in her storage wall. "Here it is."

She held up a pale, gray-blue mat. "What do you think?"

"It's wonderful," I said. I laid my watercolor on the nearest table and put the mat over it. "Perfect."

"I remembered how much gray and blue you were using," she said. "What does Cait think?"

"I haven't shown it to her since I finished it," I said. "She saw it before I put in the falcon."

"I know she's coming to the fair, she and the others."

The others.

I nearly asked which "others" she meant, but I couldn't. What if they were the same "others" Cait talked about, Cait and xiii? What if Miss Ireland was like Cait? Like me?

"I'd better hurry to first period," I said. "Is it all right if I put my painting and the mat in one of your drawers?"

"I'll do it," Miss Ireland said. She smiled at me and looked straight into my eyes.

Be safe with us, she thought, deliberate and open.

I fled, confused and suddenly frightened.

I never understood Mrs. Munson and I didn't want to try. The small glimpse I'd had of how her mind worked—all that pettiness and jealousy and spite—had been enough. So when she asked Woody to read the bulletin again, I could only believe that she was crazy, too.

"I can't read it," he complained. "I got a sore throat."

"You've been talking ever since you walked in the

door," Mrs. Munson said flatly. She handed him the bulletin, and when he refused to take it, she let it drift to his desk.

He looked up at her and she stared down at him. He got to his feet, grabbed the bulletin, and stomped to the front of the class. She smiled, satisfied.

I groaned inside. He'd stumble and bumble around, and then he'd be embarrassed and angry, and somebody would pay. I slid down in my seat and studied my folded hands.

Greg and Sam were whispering, and Mrs. Munson slammed a book down on her desk and said, "Quiet!"

I tried to think of other things while Woody trashed the English language. My fingers ached because I gripped my hands together so hard. I thought of Bingo and the quail and Jordan.

Suddenly Woody shouted, and that got my attention.

"I can't read when you're staring at me!" he yelled. "Knock it off! You want me to stop you?"

He was yelling at Althea, who leaned back in her chair, as if to get as far away from him as she could.

"Don't be rude, Althea," Mrs. Munson said.

"She wasn't staring at anybody," Julie said.

Mrs. Munson looked at Julie for a long moment and then said, "Mind your own business."

Half the class laughed. The other half sat in careful silence. Jennifer threw her head back and brayed. She'd begun laughing that way the year before, after she'd taken a modeling course. I couldn't stand to watch, so I looked out the window.

Let me be somewhere else, I thought.

. . . and there was the white horse and the earth spirit with golden grasses braided into her silver hair and a giggling crowd of tree spirits scampering in and out of an abandoned squirrel nest. I reached up to pat the horse . . .

The bell rang. Startled, I looked around to see the kids picking up their books and backpacks and shoving out the door.

"Are you okay?" Greg asked.

I smiled uncertainly.

"You didn't fall asleep, did you?" he asked quietly. "Big mistake in here."

I jumped up. "I wasn't asleep," I said.

I started toward Mitzie, who was waiting by the door, but Mrs. Munson stepped in front of me.

"Haven't you learned by now to pay attention in class?" she asked.

I tried to push past her, but she blocked my way for just a second too long, exactly the length of time for me to become afraid. Satisfied, she smiled and let me pass.

I hurried out the door with Mitzie and Julie right behind me.

"What was that all about?" Mitzie asked. "Did Munson say something to you?"

"She told me to pay attention in class."

"Why?" Julie asked. "Did she catch you looking out the window?"

Althea waited in the hall. When my gaze met hers, she smiled sadly and then turned away.

"What a great start on the day," I said as my friends and I started toward our next class.

"Every day's a party for us," Julie said sarcastically.

Halfway through lunch, Althea joined us. As usual, she didn't bring or buy food. We offered to share our lunches, but she said, "I'm not hungry. I had plenty to eat at breakfast."

Maybe she's on a diet, I thought. Maybe she was one of those people who starved themselves. But why would she care about what she weighed when she wore the same clothes day after day? I felt sorry for her, but at the same time I wished I'd never met her.

She wasn't a falcon. What a silly idea. If I wasn't careful, I'd end up locked away somewhere.

"Are there any new boys in school?" Althea asked. "Boys who weren't in your classes last year?"

"What?" Julie asked.

"Huh?" Mitzie's mouth was full.

I shrugged, mystified. "I don't know. There aren't any new sophomores that I know of."

"No sophomores," Julie said, "but there are two new

116

junior boys. They're in my chemistry class." Julie was really smart, and some of her classes were for juniors.

Althea's dark gaze never left Julie's face. "Are they here, in the cafeteria?"

Julie shook her head. "No, juniors have second lunch."

Althea got up abruptly and excused herself. As she walked away, Mitzie said, "What was that all about?"

"She's interested in boys?" I asked.

"Oh, come on," Julie said, laughing. "Everybody's interested in boys. But they don't have to be new in school."

I didn't see Althea for the rest of the day, but when Mitzie and I left school that afternoon I saw her standing across the street in the rain, watching the main doorway.

"Mitzie, I forgot something," I said. "Go on without me. I've got to go back and talk to Miss Ireland for a few minutes."

"I'll wait," Mitzie said, puzzled.

"No, it might take longer. Go ahead. I'll call you when I get home."

Mitzie ran off, pulling her hood over her head. I waited until she was nearly out of sight and then I crossed the street to Althea.

She seemed haggard, as if something terrible had happened that afternoon.

"Are you all right?" I asked.

She nodded. Her feet were wet. Her ugly brown coat seemed much too large.

"Who are you waiting for?" I asked. "Maybe I can help."

"You can't," she said.

"Tell me and maybe I can," I said. "Who are you looking for?"

She shook her head.

Even though I knew better than to involve myself, I said, "Althea, I know what you are."

"I know you do," she said quietly. "And I know what you are."

I was afraid of that. "Who are you looking for?" I asked.

Althea walked away. She didn't even look back.

I stood there stupidly while rain drenched me. It was a hard rain, sharp as steel shafts, like the one that fell when part of the cliff slid down to the Sound.

. . . The side of the cliff crumbled and fell, taking with it the ledge where the falcons had nested. The parent birds flew up crying, while one fledgling struggled free of the mud. Only one . . .

"Hey, whatcha doing out here in the weather?"

Greg held a bright green umbrella over my head.

"You look half drowned," he said. "Why are you standing here?"

I shook my head, bewildered. "I don't know. I guess I was just thinking."

"Think on your way home," he said. "Come on. I'll walk with you."

"You don't need to."

"Yes, I do. I spent twenty bucks on this magnificent umbrella and I want to try it out."

I took a good look at the green umbrella then. It was covered with the black silhouettes of frogs.

"Don't you attract a lot of snakes?" I asked.

He looked around furtively. "Is Woody here?" he asked.

I had to laugh. He laughed, too, then winced and made me feel guilty.

"You started it," I said.

He had the nicest eyes!

Before I could move away, he leaned in and kissed me quickly.

"Hey," I said, stepping back.

"That's what I thought, too," he said, grinning. "*Hey.* Now I'll take you home. I'll consider this our first date."

"Get away from me," I said, beginning to laugh. "Where did you get all that nerve?"

"I planned it all day. No, that's not true. I thought of kissing you in first period, when you started daydreaming. You looked . . . I don't know. Magical. I wanted to be where you were."

I nearly told him, but I stopped in time.

This was getting dangerous. I was beginning to have trouble telling one world from another. And talking about it to a friend might be too easy.

"Actually, I fell asleep in class, and Mitzie said I snored," I said.

Greg stepped away from me. "Quit it. You're spoiling my fantasies."

"They could use a little spoiling," I said. "I still can't get over how you got up enough nerve to kiss me. I might have socked you, you know."

"Yeah, but then I'd tell your mother."

I grinned, imagining what her reaction would be. Finally I came to my senses.

"Look, you can't walk all the way home with me and then go clear back to your place. It's too far and your ribs probably hurt. Walk me to the corner and I'll run the rest of the way."

"Nope . . ." he began.

"Yes!" I said. "I get my way because you kissed me without asking."

"Asking?" he asked. "Asking? Who does that?"

"All the boys who get to kiss me twice," I said, laughing. And then I wondered what had possessed me to say that. Maybe he'd never want to kiss me again.

We'd reached the corner by then, so I waved and ran off. When I looked back, he was still standing there, grinning foolishly. For a moment, I thought I saw something shimmering around him, a light that looked as if it might shine from deep inside a seashell or from a star a million light years away. *Greg, too?* I wondered.

I shook my head, half angry because of my fantasies, which should have been about Jordan.

I'd have given anything if I'd had that conversation with lonely, beautiful Jordan.

I fed the quail alone that afternoon. Jordan's house was dark that evening. My parents argued for an hour about buying new tires for Mom's car and never reached a decision.

The bus plunged downhill.

chapter Ten

I woke in the morning to the sound of a sudden rainstorm lashing the window. Bingo lay at the foot of my bed, watching me.

"Do you have to go out?" I asked. My throat felt sore. I wanted to pull the blankets over my head and sleep forever.

Bingo didn't seem enthusiastic about getting up, but I crawled out of bed and called to him. I could hear my parents in the kitchen as I padded barefoot down the stairs. I wasn't ready to talk to them yet, so I let Bingo out the front door.

He leaped over xiii, who crouched on the steps, rain glistening on his bright green skin.

"Good morning," xiii said cheerfully.

"Let me alone," I said.

"I like you, too," he said. "Be alert today."

"Why?"

He stared at me. "Because I said so. It's my job."

Bingo rushed back up the steps, careful to avoid xiii. I followed him inside and shut the door.

Be alert. Okay, I would. For all the good it would do.

By the time I'd showered, dressed, and got back downstairs, Mom was ready to leave. "Wear your parka or carry an umbrella," she said. "Are you all right? You look awfully pale."

"I'm okay," I said, even though my throat was definitely sore.

After she left, I joined Dad in the kitchen. The room seemed colder and darker than usual.

"Want a ride to school?" Dad asked.

I shrugged. "Sure. Can we pick up Mitzie? And Jordan?" I don't know why I added Jordan's name. We'd never given him a ride anywhere.

"They've got to be ready," Dad said. "I don't have time to wait around." He stirred as if he'd get up but he didn't.

I called Mitzie as I drank my orange juice. She was getting a ride with her mother. I called Jordan's number and heard just what I feared. A recorded voice told me that the number was no longer in service.

"So, chickie?" Dad asked, looking at me over the edge of the morning paper.

"Mitzie's got a ride and Jordan must have already left because there wasn't an answer," I lied.

But then I came to my senses. Dad should know. He might help. Some fathers would.

"Dad, I didn't get a busy signal. Jordan's number has been disconnected."

Dad looked back at his paper. "Hmm," he said. "Maybe it's out of order because of the storm."

"I think it's out of order because nobody paid the bill," I said. "I think Jordan doesn't have any money."

Dad closed his eyes for a moment, as if what I'd said hurt him. Then he looked at me sadly.

"Chickie, his father wouldn't abandon him," he said. "Don't start getting ideas. O'Neal will send money or pay the bill—or come back for Jordan. People don't just drive away and leave their children behind. Ask Jordan. Ask him what his dad's plans are."

"He always lies to me," I said bitterly. Dad! I thought in despair. Can't you hear me? Can't you understand?

"Oh, chickie," Dad said, his voice disapproving. "Why would he lie?"

"Because he's ashamed," I said. "You know that's true."

"O'Neal isn't a good father, but he wouldn't aban-don—no, no. There's got to be an explanation. You'll see. Jordan's line is out of order, and everything will be fine. Are you about ready to leave?"

There was no point in arguing. If there was anything

Dad was good it, it was avoiding an issue. I ran upstairs to get my homework, discovered that I'd forgotten to finish my French, and would have yelled something at somebody if my throat hadn't hurt so much.

We went out the front door together, and Dad brushed close to xiii, who was combing his long red hair with what looked like a grasshopper's leg. As Dad headed for his car, xiii shouted, *"Adieu, papa! Bon aventure!"*

"Shut up," I said in passing.

"What did you say, chickie?" Dad asked as he climbed into the driver's seat.

"Nothing, nothing," I said as I ran around to the passenger side. I tried to pull up my hood, failed, and felt rain soaking my hair.

What a wonderful day.

Xiii waved good-bye with the grasshopper leg.

Mitzie was waiting by our locker.

"Your hair is wet," she said when she saw me.

"Who cares? Who cares?" I said. "I always look like a freak."

"Aw, what's wrong?" she asked, concerned.

"Everything!" I shoved my parka inside the locker and banged the door shut. "Are you ready to face the ugly hag down the hall?"

"Munson?" Mitzie asked. "No, because I'm still conscious. How about you?"

125

"Dad told me once to never make eye contact with people I don't like," I said. "Maybe I'll try that."

Mitzie snorted a laugh. "She might sneak up on you."

The first bell rang and we hurried to class. Ahead of us, we saw Woody push Julie into Sam and laugh when Julie dropped her backpack. Sam picked it up for her. Woody had disappeared into the crowd. Althea skulked along wearing her sopping coat over her strange clothes.

Another stupid day at the bottom of the pit where the driverless bus was heading.

I'd barely settled into my seat when Greg leaned over my shoulder, smacked his lips, and said, "Wanna meet me after school again, babe?"

"Get away from me," I said. I was in no mood for clowning around.

He pretended to cringe. "Please don't hit me, lady," he whimpered.

After he went to his seat, Mitzie whispered, "You met him after school yesterday?"

I blushed, remembering the kiss. "No, he was standing around with this crazy umbrella he wanted to show off."

"He's so sweet," Mitzie murmured. "But I think I'm starting to like Barry Ross. Not that it'll do me any—"

"Be quiet, Mitzie!" Mrs. Munson yelled from the front of the room.

I slid down in my seat and thought of the horse that carried me through the water to the house in the woods.

"Good girl," xiii said from the lower branch of a tree that hung over the path to the house.

"Bridget, Bridget, Bridget!" the tree spirits called.

An earth spirit sang a song about me and . . .

Who?

The bell rang and the class was over. Greg grinned at me on our way out of the room.

During lunch Althea sat huddled inside her coat, staring at the bare table in front of her.

"Are you feeling all right?" I croaked. My throat really hurt by then.

She looked up at me, her dark eyes huge and haunted.

Who was she searching for? I wondered. Why was she here?

She still looked at me, waiting for me to understand. Willing me to understand.

And then I did! In the midst of thunder that only I could hear, and illuminated by lightning that only I saw, I watched her brother, the other young falcon, disappear into the mud and rock that cascaded down to the beach.

Oh, I'm so sorry! I thought.

She blinked away my sympathy. She believed he was somewhere nearby, lost to her, wandering in another form.

She thought he might be a new boy in school. She had even looked for him in the grade school.

But didn't she realize he might be dead?

She blinked again and looked away. No, the thought of him dead was unbearable.

"Hey," Mitzie said softly, nudging me. "You okay?"

"Sure," I said. I tried to swallow, and my throat hurt so much that I winced. Probably I was going crazy, and all I was worried about was a sore throat.

"You sound awful," Mitzie said. "Maybe you should go home."

"Thanks, but I'll be fine."

What had xiii said about my cut finger? It wasn't cut. I was imagining it.

In xiii's world, nothing was wrong with me.

In my world, my throat was sore.

Because you believe in everything that seems bad, xiii whispered. *Believe in everything that is good.*

I was so tired of pushing his words away, of shoving down my gifts. If for just one moment I could let myself see that everything that was real was also good . . .

Althea stood up. "Excuse me, please," she told us.

"See you later, for sure," I said, and I meant it.

My throat didn't hurt.

Was it that simple?

No, it's that *hard,* xiii whispered.

Can anyone do it? I asked him. I thought of Jordan and his troubles.

Only the Other Ones, xiii whispered. Only the real ones.

But Jordan's real! I cried silently.

Xiii didn't answer.

". . . so she told me I could go with you guys," Julie was saying. "If that's okay."

"Sure," Mitzie said. "Bridget's riding with us, too."

"What?" I asked.

Mitzie grinned. "Caught you daydreaming again, didn't we? Julie wants to ride to the art fair with us. There's plenty of room in Mom's car."

"Good," I said. I hadn't wanted to go with my parents, because I hadn't wanted to be too late or too early, or in any other way involve myself in whatever mischance they had lined up for themselves Thursday night.

Planning something with friends made my day seem normal for the first time.

In art class, Miss Ireland lingered by my drawing board. "I'm eager to see what everyone thinks of your water-color," she said. "I think it's the best thing you've done yet."

Even as she spoke she looked down at my sketch of the earth spirits. She had assigned us another study in per-spective. I expected her to frown, but she smiled instead, and moved on to Greg. She leaned down and whispered something, and he nodded.

I got up, restless and apprehensive, feeling as if a thunderstorm would begin any moment. The rain fell steadily. There was no wind. The view out the window was depressing.

Miss Ireland didn't care if we wandered around the class looking at everyone else's work. I headed toward Jordan, wondering if he'd drawn Mikey again. When I passed Althea, I glanced at her drawing. Usually she didn't do much but make vague scratches, but this time she'd made a light sketch of the roof of a house. As seen from the air.

Goosebumps broke out on my arms and I hugged myself.

I stopped behind Jordan and looked over his shoulder. He'd drawn Mikey, of course, but this time the dog was looking up, ready to leap into the sky.

I touched Jordan's arm. "I'm going out to feed the quail no matter how much it rains. Will you come?"

He didn't look up at me. "Sure," he muttered. "I guess it doesn't make any difference if I'm cold outside or cold inside."

"What?" I said.

He shook his head. "Nothing." He glanced back over his shoulder and smiled. "Don't pay attention to me."

As if I could stop, I thought.

* * *

130

Mitzie's mother took us home after school. We passed Jordan first. He walked head down, hurrying. Then we passed Althea, cringing in the terrible rain.

"Stop for her!" Mitzie cried.

But Althea, as if she'd heard Mitzie, left the road suddenly and darted across someone's front yard.

"She must be visiting someone there," Mrs. Coburn said, and she sounded puzzled.

"Who does Althea know?" Mitzie asked.

Anna, who was sitting in back with Mitzie, said, "That wasn't Althea. It was somebody in an ugly brown coat."

Mitzie sighed noisily. "Okay, have it your way."

After they dropped me off and turned back down the road, I let Bingo out. Xiii hadn't been in any of his usual places, but when I heard Bingo yelp from the side yard, I walked to the edge of the porch and saw him fleeing from the glittering dragon stalking across the grass.

Xiii looked up and saw me watching.

"Just having a little fun," he said.

I let Bingo back in the house and patted him. "Try to ignore him," I advised the dog. "Don't make eye contact."

Bingo's expression told me that it wouldn't do any good. Dragons do whatever they please.

I knocked on Jordan's door a few minutes later and he surprised me by answering immediately. We hurried through the rain to the place where the quail waited, and scattered seed and cracked corn in the clearing. We didn't stay to see them eat.

As we climbed back over the fence to Jordan's yard, I said, "Come over for dinner tonight. There's enough macaroni and cheese to feed an army."

"I don't know—" he began.

"Please," I said. "If you don't come, then we'll probably have to eat it for leftovers tomorrow. Between you and Bingo, maybe I'll get spaghetti tomorrow night instead."

Jordan laughed. "How can I turn down an invitation like that?"

I looked up and saw his rain-wet face and I wanted to smooth away the cold drops. And all his troubles, too.

"Okay, dinner's at six sharp," I said. "Don't be late, because Bingo will eat your share."

"I like macaroni and cheese," Jordan said. "I'll be on time."

I walked away grinning like an idiot. Jordan was coming for dinner!

And my parents would hate that.

My grin faded.

Xiii was washing vigorously in the rain pouring over the edge of the roof gutter. "You've complicated what could have been a simple situation," he said.

I stopped. "What's that supposed to mean?"

He scraped his chest with a dragon scale and I thought for a moment that he wasn't going to answer. But then he turned on me in a fury.

"If you want to help him, then *help* him!" he yelled. Quick as a blink, he changed to a frog and then a white parrot.

"Now look what you've done!" he squawked.

He turned back into the mean little red-haired boy.

"Bridget," he said, and he made my name sound almost like a whine. "Think. Try it just once and see what happens."

The dragon scale lay on the path in front of him. I concentrated, lifted my hand, and the scale rose in the air. Then, with a flick of my wrist, I made the scale sail through the rain to the road.

"Congratulations," xiii said. "You look like an idiot."

With that, he disappeared.

I went inside to take the macaroni and cheese out of the freezer. Bingo rolled his eyes at me as I passed him.

"Don't say it," I said.

Mom came in a few minutes later and tossed her raincoat over the back of the kitchen stool. "I left early because of the storm," she said. "Oh, good, you took out the macaroni and cheese. That sounds good on a rotten day like this."

"I invited Jordan to come over for dinner," I said.

She stared at me. "What?" she asked.

I repeated myself, and added, "I don't think he eats much when his father is out of town." I looked down at the tomato I was slicing. "Actually," I said cautiously, "I've got an awful feeling that Jordan ran out of money. Maybe he's not eating at all. Maybe we ought to do something."

"That's ridiculous," Mom said sharply. "His father wouldn't have left him without enough money for food."

"He left him without enough money to keep the phone working," I said. I wouldn't look up because I knew what I'd see on her face.

"You're worrying about nothing," Mom said. "No one would leave a boy in a house without . . ."

I looked at her then. "Without a phone? Well, that would be mean, because he might have an emergency. But what if he did? And what if Jordan doesn't even have money for food? What if his father never comes back? Isn't somebody supposed to care?"

"His friends—" Mom began.

"*I'm* his friend. He doesn't have any others."

"The school—"

"Doesn't care! Nobody cares!"

"Don't use that tone with me," Mom said.

I went back to the tomato, my life's work, and sliced carefully.

"Nobody cares," I repeated.

I heard Mom tapping her foot. "I take it that you think we should do something. Interfere in some way. What did you have in mind? Taking him in here? Calling the police? Reporting your worries to the school?"

"Any of the above," I said. I sliced a radish, hard as my mother's heart.

"People get in trouble that way," she said. "Jordan's what? Sixteen? He's old enough to call his father or one of his relatives if he's really in trouble."

"What if there isn't anyone? What then?"

"There's a guidance counselor at school," she said. "If what you say is true, then why doesn't he—"

"Tell the school that his father didn't think enough of him to make sure he had food and a warm house and a phone? I wouldn't tell. I wouldn't want anyone to know that my father didn't care about me any more than that."

Suddenly I began to cry. Now my sore throat was back and worse than ever, and crying really hurt. I pulled a paper towel off the roll and wiped my eyes, but they teared up again. My sobs were childish and noisy.

Bingo left the room.

"For heaven's sake, stop it," Mom said. "All right. Jordan's coming over for dinner. We'll find a way of asking about his father. You'll see. You're behaving this way for no good reason."

She started toward the door to the dining room and then turned back.

"Don't ask anyone here for dinner again without talking to me first," she said.

"Okay," I said.

When she was gone, I sliced a radish neatly in two pieces and threw both of them into the garbage can under the sink.

chapter Eleven

When Dad got home, I let Mom tell him that Jordan was coming to dinner. Dad didn't say anything to me. He sat down in the living room and watched the TV news.

I set the table and put out olives and applesauce, two things I liked to eat with macaroni and cheese. Mom silently defrosted rolls and poured water into glasses.

At six exactly, Jordan knocked on our front door. Bingo barked ecstatically when I let Jordan in, and it took a few minutes for him to settle down.

Dad looked away from the TV long enough to say, "Hello there," to Jordan.

Mom didn't come out of the kitchen.

Jordan had changed clothes and wore a dark blue cardigan over a white T-shirt. I was sorry I hadn't changed out of the clothes I'd worn to school. I hadn't even brushed my hair.

Great start, I told myself.

"Dinner will be ready in about ninety seconds," I told Jordan. "Why don't you just sit down at the table?"

"Sure," he said. I pointed out the chair I wanted him to take and then rushed out to the kitchen.

"Jordan's here," I told Mom. "I'll take the macaroni out of the oven."

"I'll bring in coffee for your dad," she said.

My mouth was dry. I was worried that the dinner would be awful or that my parents would behave rudely, although they never had before when my friends were in the house.

I carried the macaroni to the table and set it down in the middle on the cork pad I'd put there earlier.

"Oh, gosh," Jordan said simply.

"Smells good, doesn't it?" I said. "I didn't make it, though. Do you want milk, or is water enough?"

"Milk sounds great," he said.

I ran to get milk for him, bumped my shoulder into the door frame, and nearly stepped on Bingo. Mom, watching me, rolled her eyes.

I don't care, I thought. This will turn out all right, no matter how clumsy and stupid I am.

Dad shuffled in just as I brought Jordan's milk to the

table. "Everything looks wonderful," he said as he sat down.

Mom sat at the other end of the table. She still hadn't spoken to Jordan.

"The dinner looks good, Mrs. Raynes," Jordan said.

"Thank you, Jordan," Mom said. She smiled a little.

Oh please, I begged xiii or anything else that might have been listening to my thoughts at that moment. Make this be all right.

Mom told Jordan that we served ourselves from casseroles and she told him to start. He didn't take as much as I thought he wanted, but I'd urge him to take more when he'd finished that. I passed rolls and butter to him. When the applesauce reached Jordan, Dad said, "Take plenty, Jordan. I'm not fond of it myself, but Bridget loves it."

"So do I," Jordan said.

When our plates were full, Dad said, "Jordan, I heard on the radio when I was driving home that some people are worried about another landslide. What do you think?"

I saw Jordan blink. Then he said, "The slides last spring were pretty bad."

"Bridget tells me there's someone living in that house on the cliff," Dad said.

"The new girl in school," Jordan said.

"Her parents think the house is safe," I said. "I walked home with her once and met them."

Out of the corner of my eye I saw Mom looking at me.

"What kind of people are they?" she asked.

They're actually *falcons,* I thought, and I longed to say it just to see what she'd do. "They seemed nice enough," I said vaguely. "Sort of quiet."

"I wish you wouldn't go into strangers' houses," Mom said. She poked at her salad. "You never know what might happen."

Better change the subject fast, I told myself. Otherwise, Jordan would know more than any rational person would want to know about this runaway bus I was on.

"The art fair is coming up the day after tomorrow," I said. "It should be interesting this year."

"It was lovely last year," Mom said. "Have you entered your watercolor yet, Bridget?"

"Sure," I said. I buttered a roll. "I think Greg will win. He did a wonderful painting of the beach."

"He's a smart boy," Dad said. He helped himself to more macaroni and cheese. "Ready for seconds, Jordan?"

This *could* work out, I thought.

"How's your dad?" Dad asked Jordan. "Any word about when he's coming back?"

Jordan, caught with his fork in midair, froze. Finally he said, "The job is taking longer than he thought."

Dad nodded as if this answered everything. "That's a shame. But I suppose you're keeping busy over there."

"Sure," Jordan said quietly.

"When was the last time you heard from him?" Mom asked. "Does he know about this awful weather?"

"Oh, sure, I told him," Jordan said. He concentrated on his plate.

Dad immediately began talking about football.

When we finished eating, Mom helped me clear the table. When we were in the kitchen, she whispered, "See? I told you everything was all right."

I rubbed my forehead where a small, mean headache was beginning. "You didn't find out anything. You didn't ask the right questions."

"And what are the right questions?" Mom hissed. She didn't wait for an answer but went back to the dining room with the coffee pot to refill Dad's cup.

"I think I'll have my second cup in the living room," Dad said. "Care to join me, Jordan?"

Jordan looked at me. I wanted to shout, "No, don't go, not until you've told us what's happening to you." But I only smiled.

"I'd probably better start home," Jordan said. "I've got a lot of homework tonight."

He thanked Mom and Dad twice for having him over for dinner. I walked to the door with him and he thanked me.

141

"This was great," he said. "Maybe someday, after Dad gets back . . ."

No one could see us. I touched his arm.

"Jordan, can I help?" I asked quietly.

His face flushed. "See you tomorrow, Bridget," he said, and he ran down the porch steps, into the rain.

Xiii watched him leave. "Nice try," he told me from the shelter of the moss rose. "You know what he needs. You're supposed to take care of it. That's why you're here. To help, not to stand around on the sidelines bawling over nightmares."

I couldn't hear Jordan's footsteps any longer. He'd reached his dark, cold, empty house.

"I don't know what to do to help him," I told xiii.

He hopped closer to the porch. "Come to the woods tonight and you'll see," he said.

"See what?"

But he was gone again.

I wasn't about to go to the woods at night. I was afraid of what I'd find there.

The Other Ones.

And if I did, would I come back the same person I'd been when I went? Or would I start a life I didn't want?

If I accepted myself as what Cait said I was, would I be able to change my mind if I hated it? If I couldn't bear the loneliness? If I lost any chance I ever had of being accepted?

I went inside and shut the door.

Dad glanced away from the TV. "See? Everything's just fine over at Jordan's house. He had plenty of opportunity to tell us if something was wrong."

"Sure," I said bitterly.

In the kitchen, Mom was fixing Bingo's dinner. I leaned against the counter and drew circles on the damp tiles. "Tell me what you'd do if you were sixteen and your father left you alone without money or anyone to help you," I said. "Would you want to tell the neighbors what a rotten family you came from? Over macaroni and cheese?"

"Your father asked him—"

"Would you tell the neighbors?" I shouted.

Mom put down the spoon she'd been holding. "Don't use that tone with me. Maybe you'd better go to your room and calm down. If you still believe that Jordan has been abandoned, then tell the guidance counselor at school tomorrow. After all the trouble you've had with bullies and your English teacher, he's not likely to be astonished by anything you say."

I walked out without answering and went to my room. For a long time I sat on the edge of my bed, thinking about what Mom had said. Yes, I could go to the guidance counselor and tell him I thought Jordan had been abandoned. He'd call Jordan in and ask him, and Jordan would lie. Then Jordan would never speak to me again.

And he'd still have his problems.

I got up and pushed open my window. Rain fell in sheets, and I could smell the woods.

"You're starting to figure things out," xiii whispered.

"No, I'm not," I cried. I batted at the owl sitting on my windowsill. "I wish you'd either tell me what you know or leave me alone. You're always nagging! And following me around! I thought you were supposed to be a threshold guardian. Why don't you stay here all the time then, guarding the *threshold,* instead of snooping after me?"

The owl drew close. "I go with you because you are the threshold, Bridget. *You are the threshold.*"

I stared at him. "What are you talking about?"

"If you're willing, I'll come back for you late tonight and take you to a place in the woods where you'll meet the Others."

"If I go, can I come back?" I asked, frightened.

The owl shook his feathers, preparing for flight. "Of course you can come back. You're *supposed* to come back."

"But I'll be different," I said. "And everybody will know, just the way they know about Cait."

But the owl flew out into the rain.

"Xiii!" I hissed after him.

He didn't return, and I closed my window. I wasn't willing to go to the woods.

*   *   *

Even though it was late, my parents decided they wanted to rent a video, so they left for the grocery store. I tried to finish my homework but couldn't concentrate. I needed to talk to someone.

Mitzie? No. I'd tell her the next morning about Jordan, but nothing else.

Cait.

I called my aunt. She was laughing when she picked up the phone.

"I'm sorry!" I said. "You've got guests."

"No, no," she said. "The cats and I were watching one of those British comedies they like so much."

I couldn't help laughing. "I almost believe you," I said.

"Are you feeling better?" she asked.

I swallowed and it hurt. "I think I'm catching a cold."

"You don't need to," Cait said. "When you hang up, fix yourself a cup of tea and listen to quiet music for a while. Focus on the moment. You'll feel better, I promise."

"Cait," I said. "Xiii wants me to go to the woods tonight."

"Of course," she said. "You're welcome whenever you want to come."

She wasn't surprised!

"Who else will be there?" I asked.

"Oh, the cats and I, and a few others."

"The Other Ones," I said. I began pleating the top sheet on the message pad beside the phone. I was sorry I'd called.

"Yes, Bridget. Just us."

"Do I know any of them?" I asked.

"Do *you* think you do?" she asked.

I thought of Miss Ireland. "Maybe," I said. I tore the sheet of paper off and crumpled it.

Cait laughed gently. "Bridget, they're family. You'll be safer than you've ever been. And if you come, I'll know you're ready."

"Xiii told me tonight that I'm the threshold he's guarding," I said. I clenched my hand around the phone.

I could hear one of the cats purring into the phone. "We trust his judgment to tell you what you need to know," Cait said.

I nearly growled. "*I* don't trust him. Sometimes I can't stand him. Do you have a guardian? Why haven't I ever seen him?"

"You won't need one after you accept," she said.

A life without xiii? I couldn't imagine such a thing. I'd be relieved, but . . . Who would I have to argue with?

"It will be all right, Bridget," Cait said. "I promise. Now, I want you to fix that tea, and I'll see you Thursday evening at the art fair. All right?"

"Yes, all right," I said. "Cait?"

"What is it?"

"Were you afraid that first night?"

"I was terrified," she said. "When I went out to meet the Others the first time, I had no idea what to expect. But they were wonderful. Healing. I knew I was with the best friends I'd ever have."

I told her good-bye and hung up. On my way to the kitchen, I wondered if I'd have familiars. Bingo, plodding behind me, didn't seem to be a possibility.

I fixed the tea, carried it upstairs, and played soft music on my stereo while I sat with a mohair teddy bear on my lap. I focused as Cait had told me to do. After a while, when I felt better, I went to bed.

I dreamed of Jordan walking with me on a warm beach somewhere on the other side of the world. Or perhaps on a different planet. I didn't want to wake up.

The rain stopped during the night, and after breakfast, I walked to Mitzie's house. My sore throat was gone, but I was tired. My backpack cut into my shoulders. I wished it were Friday instead of only Wednesday, especially since Friday was an in-service day for the teachers, so we had the day off.

Mitzie ran out when she saw me coming. "I thought the rain would never stop," she said. "We heard on the radio that there was a landslide on Three Firs Road, so it's closed. I know I shouldn't be glad, but that means Jennifer won't make it to school today."

I snickered. "Gosh, what a tragedy. Listen, last night Jordan came over for dinner."

Mitzie stopped to stare at me. "You're kidding! You got up enough nerve to ask him?"

My smile faded. "I thought I'd better. I have a hunch that he's run out of money and isn't eating."

Mitzie walked on, head down, thinking. "That's awful," she said finally. "Somebody's got to do something."

"That's what I told my parents, but they don't want to get involved. They think he'd go talk to Ziegler if he was really in trouble."

Mitzie burst out laughing. "They really said that?"

"Mom did."

"She's met Ziegler, too," Mitzie said, marveling. "I wouldn't tell anybody at school anything that mattered."

"But what would you do if you were left alone without money?" I asked.

Mitzie shook her head. "My parents wouldn't do that, not even to Anna." She paused. "But Mr. O'Neal would."

"I asked Jordan before he left if I could help him, but I embarrassed him," I said.

Mitzie understood that. "He doesn't want to look like nobody cares about him. It would be hard to admit."

"Impossible," I said. "What should I do?"

"Let me think about it," Mitzie said slowly. "Maybe I

could talk to Mom about it. She knows lots of people."

"But what if Jordan finds out that I started all this? He'd really resent me."

"That's better than his going hungry, Bridget," Mitzie said.

My face burned. "You're right. But give me one more day to see what I can find out. If I'm wrong, and Jordan has plenty to eat and his dad is really coming back, then at least I won't embarrass him."

Far ahead of us, Althea drifted along on the rain-soaked grass beside the road. Mitzie and I watched her, but neither of us said anything, until Mitzie finally blurted, "Anna makes me furious. I don't believe for one minute that she knows who Althea is."

"Right," I said.

I traveled with the white horse during first period, in perfect, warm peace. I saw a group of girls harvesting flowers in a long field that sloped down to the cold sea. Tree spirits brought me fresh honey on curled red leaves. A boy I almost recognized held the horse's head when I slipped down to investigate a rock imbedded with silver symbols I couldn't read. When the bell rang, I was still smiling.

As Mitzie and I left the classroom, Greg brushed his hand against my arm and said, "Nice."

* * *

The rain began again that afternoon and brought with it a wild windstorm. A little after one o'clock, the power went out, so we were sent home. Mitzie and I fled to her house with the cold shafts of rain pelting us. Ahead, through the downpour, I saw Jordan running for home. Althea struggled against the wind, her thin body outlined inside the ugly brown coat, and I wondered if she was cold.

"Quick, quick," Mitzie gasped, pulling my sleeve. "You can't stand out here watching Althea."

"I feel sorry for her," I said.

"Do you want me to run after her and see if she wants to come in?" Mitzie asked.

I shook my head sadly. "She won't."

"Let's make hot chocolate," Mitzie said. "We'll feel better about everything then."

Anna was in the kitchen with her mother, and when we walked in, she scowled. "Is the high school out, too?" she asked.

"What a terrible day," Mrs. Coburn said. "The clerk in the grocery store told me that a train was derailed a few miles from here. Another landslide."

I thought of Althea in her house perched on the cliff, and what she had lost in the spring landslides. "Maybe the rain will quit pretty soon," I said.

The rain did let up for a while later in the afternoon,

giving me enough time to rush home. Xiii, wearing a crabby expression and a maple leaf for a cape, sat on the gate.

"I thought you never got cold," I said as I passed him.

He dropped to the ground and scampered ahead of me, tossing off the maple leaf as he went. "So you liked the white horse enough to call her back again," he said.

"No thanks to you," I said as I climbed the steps.

"*All* thanks to me!" xiii shouted. "You ungrateful, selfish daughter of misery and wickedness! I called up that horse for you!"

I'd been reaching for the doorknob, but I stopped. "You did not!" I said. "I called her up myself!"

Xiii grinned slyly up at me. "Well, well," he said. "The brat's finally admitted it."

I shoved open the door and let Bingo out. He hadn't barked and I wasn't certain he'd been waiting on the other side of the door, but from the way he rushed past xiii, I understood that he was smart enough not to interrupt.

"So you're coming tonight?" xiii asked.

"No," I said. "I'm doing fine just as I am."

Xiii let out a squawk that sounded like a furious hen. "What can be done with you?"

"Just let me alone," I said. Bingo rushed back into the house and didn't wait to see if I'd follow.

"I can't leave you alone," xiii whined. "I have to look out for you."

I shut the door and listened while he nattered on and on about his duties. Probably, I thought, I truly was crazy, and everybody who thought that about me was right.

chapter Twelve

I made two big sandwiches and put them in a sack with a double handful of cookies. Then I filled a container with bird seed and ran across the street, hoping Jordan would see me coming. He didn't come out, so I knocked on his door. When he opened it, I held up the container and said, "Time to feed our friends."

He brought cracked corn and we headed toward the fence at the back of his yard. The storm had stripped leaves from the trees and the world around us looked depressed and afflicted. Jordan was coughing, and he sounded as miserable as the world looked.

"How are you feeling?" I asked.

"Fine," he said. "What's in the sack?"

I handed it to him so I could climb over the fence. "I

brought a snack. I'm so hungry I can't wait for dinner. Would you like some?"

"Not if you're hungry," he said.

"I brought enough for two," I said. "It would be rude to eat in front of you and not share."

As we walked, I dug out the sandwiches. Jordan took his politely, not grabbing as I would have if I'd been as hungry as I suspected he was.

Maybe I'd been wrong about him.

But he'd eaten every crumb before we reached the stump, so I handed him the sack. "There are cookies in the bottom," I said. "You eat them. I made the sandwiches too big, and I'm full now."

"Are you sure?" he asked.

"Hey, I wouldn't offer unless I was sure," I said. "Nobody ever accused me of being generous."

He looked at me strangely. "I think you're generous. Who said you aren't?"

I didn't think telling him about xiii was especially smart.

"I see the quail," I said, and he didn't speak again. We scattered our seeds and climbed up on the stump.

The large male quail wasn't limping anymore. In spite of the terrible weather, he'd managed to heal. I should have practiced casting circles until I could do it right.

No time like this very minute, I thought, and I concentrated all my attention on the quail. In my mind, I saw a line of bright light surround them as if I had drawn it with a pencil. I focused and the line sprang up into a wall, blazing over the heads of the birds. I concentrated harder and the wall shot up to the tops of the trees, spilling crystal sparks. I closed it over the top of the quail, so that they were sealed inside and safe from everything that could harm them.

I blinked and the wall vanished from my sight, but I knew it was still there because I could hear it humming that clear, high note I remembered from my childhood when I had protected birds this same way.

It was all so easy. And so *wrong!*

The quail crept away and disappeared into the brambles.

"They look pretty good, considering the storm," Jordan said.

He had finished the last of the cookies and handed the sack to me. "I'm sorry I ate everything," he said. "I didn't know I was so hungry."

"School lunches don't stick with me very long," I told him. "I think the cafeteria makes them out of plastic."

Jordan laughed a little, then began coughing again. "The lasagna is awful. Somebody should tell them."

"Everybody tells them," I said.

We parted in his backyard. "I'm glad you came for dinner last night," I said.

"Sure," he said vaguely. He glanced around, then

155

looked straight at me. "See you tomorrow," he said. "I hope you win first prize at the art fair."

"I'll be glad to get honorable mention," I told him. "But thanks, anyway."

He went inside and I walked home, smiling. Maybe I could keep Jordan fed without anyone knowing what I was doing, not even Jordan himself. But would a sandwich a day be enough? Of course not.

I'd think of something.

Xiii waited on the porch. "Feeding him is better than nothing," he said. "But—"

"Don't," I said, and I went inside.

My parents argued all through dinner about the tires again. I wanted to tell them that McMurphy's Garage was no better than the Roadside Garage, and who cared which owner had bought shrubs from the garden store. No one asked for my opinion.

I went upstairs as soon as I finished helping Mom with the dishes and started my homework. Mitzie called me to say that she hated the English assignment, and I agreed. Who wanted to write an essay about the value of school?

"She'll make me read mine aloud," I said. "I can feel it in my bones."

"Maybe she'll make Woody read his," Mitzie said.

That idea made me laugh.

*   *   *

I'd been in bed an hour when I heard xiii whispering on my windowsill. I opened the window and found the owl perched there again.

"Come to the woods tonight," he said. "It's important that you decide."

"I've decided," I said. "I don't want to do it."

"Trouble is coming!" he said urgently. "I've warned you and warned you."

"It's always *nothing*," I said. "At least, it's not something important."

"The injury to your head was nothing?"

"I'm fine now." I began closing the window.

"Trouble!" he said. "Trouble is coming and you must be prepared! I saw what you did for the quail."

I shut the window and went back to bed.

The rain began the next morning while I fed the quail. It was a light rain, but the kind that penetrates everything. It fell steadily while I walked to Mitzie's house and chilled us to the bone before we reached school.

"This is landslide weather, Dad says," Mitzie told me.

"I believe it."

Althea reached class before we did and sat huddled inside her coat. She looked cold and ill.

Julie was picked to read the morning bulletin. Mrs. Munson glared at her until Julie began stuttering and Woody laughed.

I looked out the window until the white horse came. Distantly, I heard Sam reading his essay. The horse stopped beside a rosebush that climbed up a tree and I reached out to pick a full-blown flower. The scent . . .

The bell rang and I could still smell the rose.

"Lucky us," Mitzie said. "But poor Sam."

Greg passed us and touched me again. "Nice," he said again.

Mitzie didn't hear him.

I tried to forget him.

Althea didn't sit with us in the cafeteria. Julie said she'd seen her leaving the building.

"Maybe she's sick," Mitzie said.

Maybe she's given up, I thought. But I was wrong.

Jordan coughed so much and so deeply in art class that Miss Ireland stopped by his drawing board and murmured something to him. He got up and left. I hoped he was going to the nurse. With luck, she'd ask him questions and find out what was wrong at his house. But I couldn't count on that. I couldn't remember a time when anybody went to the nurse's office and came back with anything good to say.

On the way home, Mitzie told me her mother would pick me up at a quarter to seven. "We'll be there in plenty of time to walk around before the crowd gets there," she said. "I bet we'll find the blue ribbon on your painting."

"I wish I could be in the room when the judges decide," I told her. "Oh, not because I think they'll pick my painting. I only wonder what they say about everything. Aren't you curious?"

"Me?" Mitzie asked, laughing. "I wouldn't enter something in the art fair if my life depended on it. I hate losing."

"It's not exactly fun," I admitted. "But I like seeing Greg win."

"Oh, Greg," she said. "He's so sweet."

You have no idea, I thought, and then I wondered where *that* came from.

I fed the quail alone, and on my way back I stopped by Jordan's, hoping he'd come to the door when I knocked. He didn't, and I thought I could hear him coughing inside. I wasn't certain, though. I carried my sack of sandwiches away.

When I reached my front walk, xiii waited under the moss rose.

"He's sick," xiii said.

"I know," I said, and I kept walking.

He hopped past me and sat on the third step from the bottom. "Don't you *feel* anything?" he asked. "Don't you want to help?"

159

"Of course I do," I said. "I want to help him in a normal way, not in some weird way I don't understand that probably won't do any real good anyway."

Xiii didn't follow me. He didn't say another word. When I turned around to look, he was gone.

I went inside feeling strange, almost as if I'd lost something valuable. Or misplaced a part of myself.

Mom and I fixed dinner together and had it on the table faster than usual. Dad brought home a bottle of sparkling cider to celebrate the art fair, "Even if you don't get the first prize."

"She's going to win," Mom said firmly.

"Mom, I think Greg's going to get it again. He's better than I am."

"We'll see," she said.

I wondered if she really believed it.

Mitzie's mother came right on time, and I ran out to climb in the car with Mitzie and Julie.

"Are you excited?" Julie asked.

"For Greg," I said. I knew he'd win, and I didn't feel the least bit jealous. Someday he'd be a professional artist, just as he'd planned. I had no idea what I'd be—except that I wasn't going to be what Cait thought I'd be.

We weren't the first ones in the cafeteria, where the art fair was being held. A few students were there, ones who had entered their work. A dozen parents lingered in the doorway talking to Miss Ireland.

"Come on," Mitzie said. "Let's go look."

But I could see from across the room that the blue ribbon hung on the wall beside Greg's wonderful painting of a beach.

The white ribbon hung beside my four-seasons watercolor.

"I'm so sorry," Julie said.

"Hey, I'm glad I got the third prize," I said. "I really mean it."

Greg came in with his parents and grandparents. They hurried across the room to stand in a half circle around Greg's work. Miss Ireland joined them.

I watched, pleased. When my parents arrived, they told me they were sorry I'd lost but they didn't bother congratulating Greg. They talked to Mitzie's parents for a few minutes and then found a place to sit. Behind them, sitting at a table alone, Althea watched people come and go.

I slipped between Greg's relatives to congratulate him and tell him again that I thought his painting was wonderful.

"It's luck, you know," he said. "Just luck."

"He won't believe how talented he is," his mother said proudly.

"I know," I said.

Cait arrived then, with two women and a man I didn't

know. She introduced them as instructors at the college. They examined my painting for a long time and the man said I did fine work.

"That peregrine looks real enough to fly off the paper," he said.

Was he one of the Other Ones?

No, he was just a teacher named George Oliver.

Cait and her friends moved to Greg's painting then, and talked to him and Miss Ireland for several minutes. Greg's parents drew back. I could see they didn't like Cait or the people she was with. But one of Cait's friends patted Miss Ireland's shoulder and nodded to her.

A gang of kids charged into the cafeteria, making so much noise that everybody turned around.

Woody and his friends. What did they know or care about art? I grew angry just seeing them, and even angrier when they turned their attention to the paintings on the walls. They were going to start something and do their best to spoil the art fair. They couldn't leave anything alone!

Mitzie and Julie drew close to me when the kids gathered around my painting. I hated Woody so much that my hands were shaking.

"What's this, a picture of chickens?" Woody yelled, and he looked around to see who appreciated his joke. His friends laughed raucously.

Woody make chicken noises. "Hey, Bridget, is this *your*

chicken?" He touched the peregrine in my painting with a dirty finger. I wanted to slap his hand away.

Then I saw Althea standing nearby, alone and watching, watching.

Trouble is coming, xiii had said.

Go away, Althea, I thought suddenly, desperately. *Go away now!*

But she didn't. She couldn't seem to pull her gaze from Woody.

"Hey, Bridget, is this a chicken?" Woody yelled again.

Miss Ireland moved toward him, but I was closer. I stepped forward and said angrily, "It's a peregrine falcon."

Woody's expression changed to one of intense interest. He leaned toward me a little. "It's a falcon?" he asked. "Who'd know that? It looks like a chicken to me. Look at the feet. You want to see a falcon's foot, I'll show you one. I'll show you my lucky charm."

It happened in slow motion, each movement dragged out to last a lifetime, an eternity. Woody slid his hand into his pocket. He pulled out something. He held out his hand.

I heard Althea catch her breath, then groan.

Woody dangled the dried falcon's foot in my face. "I found the bird flopping around on the beach," he said. "I cut off—"

"Shut up!" I screamed. I tried to reach him. I wanted to scratch his eyes out, but Mitzie grabbed me.

163

"Don't," she said. "He's disgusting. He isn't worth it."

"Chicken!" Woody yelled at me, laughing. He waved the dried claw.

Rage burned through me. I gathered my strength and in my mind, I forced the claw slowly into the palm of Woody's hand, farther and farther, until it pierced his skin and he cried out. I forced it harder. *Now!* Blood spurted and flew. I wanted to shout out my victory.

Whining, Woody held out his hand, with one of the falcon's claws stuck deep in his palm.

I saw Cait.

I saw Greg.

Greg reached Woody first and pulled out the claw.

"Jeez, Woody, why don't you grow up?" he asked calmly. He held the dried foot behind his back. "You'd better go home and wash off your hand. You could get an infection."

Woody pressed his hand against his chest. "Leave me alone," he said.

"Only trying to help," Greg said soothingly. "Let me—"

"Get away from me!" Woody yelled.

"Yeah, get back!" one of his friends shouted. Cait, eyes fixed on me, moved to Greg's side just as the other boy shoved him hard.

"Hey!" Greg cried, and winced. I was afraid the other boy had hurt his cracked rib.

Cait raised one hand slightly, a small gesture that almost no one would notice. The boy turned away to join his friends, who had gathered around Woody. One of them said they'd take him home. When he left, Woody looked back at me as if he couldn't help himself. I smiled viciously and he winced with fresh pain.

Cait leaned close to me and said softly, "Stop it. The moment he came in, you entered his world. You knew there was a better way. Go sit down."

I obeyed. Mitzie and Julie hadn't heard her, but they went with me, and I couldn't decide whether they were ready to laugh or cry.

"Did you see what happened?" Julie asked. "He practically impaled himself on that claw. It serves him right after what he did to the falcon."

"Why did Greg help him?" Mitzie asked angrily.

I shook my head, but I knew. Greg paid my debt by helping his worst enemy and endangering himself.

My parents, shocked, joined us and said they wanted to leave. "Woody is worse than I thought," Mom said. "That was the most repulsive thing I've ever seen. I'm not sorry he hurt himself."

I remembered Althea and looked around. Where was she?

I jumped up. "Where's Althea?" I asked.

My friends looked around, puzzled. "She was here," Julie said.

"I wish . . ." I began.

A few feet away, Cait turned and stared at me.

Miss Ireland was wiping up the blood with paper towels. People began talking again, and in a few moments it seemed as if nothing had happened. The blood and Woody and the claw were gone.

Cait moved smoothly to my parents and said, "Isn't Bridget's painting wonderful? She gets better all the time, doesn't she?"

"We hoped she'd win," Mom said, sounding disappointed.

Miss Ireland, on her way back from getting rid of the bloody paper towels, stopped to congratulate me and say a few polite words to my parents. She smiled at me, but there was something in her eyes, something regretful.

She knows what I did, I thought.

And Greg paid the price.

I looked around to see where Greg was, but he was lost in the crowd. I needed to say something to him, but I didn't know what.

I told Mitzie I'd go home with Mom and Dad. "Tell your mom thanks for the ride," I said. "It was nice of her."

"Oh, gee, she's always glad to take you with us," Mitzie said. "Hasn't this been something? But why would Greg help that rotten Woody after Woody cracked his rib?"

I shrugged. "He's nicer than anybody else," I said.

166

Dad lifted my painting down from the wall and Mom took my white ribbon. The three of us left in silence.

I hadn't seen Althea again, and I hadn't seen the falcon's foot. I was glad to sit in the back seat so I could cry without being seen. Althea's brother . . .

I bent my head, bitter and confused.

chapter Thirteen

When we reached home, I had to persuade Dad not to hang my watercolor in the dining room right away. I didn't want to look at the peregrine. I didn't want to think of what might be happening to Althea now.

Dad put the painting in the front closet. "We'll have it properly framed and then decide where to hang it later," he told me.

"Sure, Dad," I said as I went upstairs with Bingo. I was fairly certain that Dad would forget about the painting soon. He forgot most things having to do with me in a day or so.

I had homework, but I didn't care. It wasn't due until Monday. I left my clothes on the floor, something I never did, pulled on my pajamas, crawled into bed, and turned out my bedside lamp. I hoped I'd fall asleep.

But if I couldn't, I hoped I wouldn't cry.

I wondered if Jordan was feeling better. His cough was terrible. If he didn't have money for food, then what would he do if he had to see a doctor? I got up again, opened my curtains, and stared out into the dark, windy night.

Xiii fluttered to the windowsill. I opened the window and asked, "Will Jordan get well?"

"He's alone in the dark, running a fever and in pain. Are you satisfied?"

I gritted my teeth. "What am I supposed to do? If I tell someone at school . . ."

"Set him free," xiii said.

I shook my head. "I don't know what you're talking about."

The owl ruffled his feathers, preparing to fly away again. "The dream that someone else dreamed for him is ending."

He flew away on the wind.

"Come back!" I cried. "I don't know what you mean! You have to come back."

But he didn't. I went to bed and lay awake and cold, listening. My parents came upstairs and went to bed. The house creaked in the wind. Bingo, tired of my tossing and turning, left my room.

Jordan, be well, I thought. On Monday I'll tell Mr. Ziegler and the nurse about you. I'll tell everybody. . . .

The dream that someone else dreamed for him is ending.

What about Althea? I turned over again, and pulled my knees to my chest. What about the shape-shifter? She knew now what had happened to her brother. Had she gone home and told her parents? It was unbearable to think of it.

Woody!

My fists clenched, but then I remembered Cait's face at the art fair. And the expression in Miss Ireland's eyes.

No, I won't wish him more harm, I thought. I could do it. I could hurt him again. But someone would pay a price for me. Perhaps Greg again.

Greg. He was one of the Other Ones. Would he be in the woods with them?

Did he know the things that they knew?

The dream that someone else dreamed for Jordan is ending.

Who dared to dream for him? Who had left him in this nightmare? His uncaring, ignorant father?

Then *I'll* find the real world for Jordan, I thought. I'll find the way and take him there.

I knew where I had to go to learn how.

I got out of bed, shuddering when my feet touched the cold floor. I pulled the gold robe from the closet and put it on, then opened the window. The wind roared in the trees. I leaned out into it.

"I'll go," I said quietly, knowing that xiii would hear me.

I left the house as I had once before, barefoot and

alone. Xiii flew ahead of me, leading me around the side of my house and into the thin strip of trees, all that was left of the forest that had been cut down by the builders.

But the forest was there again. No, it was different. It was older, an ancient forest, with trees so high that I couldn't see the tops. Xiii flew between tree trunks while a strange dawn broke over us, a dawn without a sun, a pale pearl of a dawn filled with the warmth of early summer and the scent of moss and ferns. The wind had died away. I heard tree spirits chattering, and an earth spirit weaving my name into a long, happy song that didn't seem to end.

Xiii perched on the back of the white horse. She twitched her ears and turned her head to look at him with mild surprise.

"Good-bye, brat," xiii said, and the horse stepped forward, carrying him into the shadows.

"Aren't you coming with me?" I asked, close to panic.

"You made a decision. My work is done."

The horse carried him away.

I walked on toward a clearing I saw through the trees, a clearing that seemed bright with sunlight in this place where there was no sun.

"Bridget is here," the earth spirit sang.

"It's Bridget, Bridget," the tree spirits called.

"Come and stand with me," Cait said.

She wore a long tunic the color of coral gleaming in

deep water, and her earrings were opals. The cats strolled behind her, whispering, surrounded by silver dust.

I took my place beside her, and a line of people passed us, each one greeting her and then smiling while she introduced me, saying, "This is our sister, our friend."

Miss Ireland came, wearing yellow silk embroidered with magical symbols. A small white dog scampered beside her. Mr. Oliver, the man at the art fair, came dressed in a khaki shirt and pants, with a small brown monkey on his shoulder.

Greg came, looking the way he usually did, wearing jeans and a sweatshirt spattered with paint. A limber ferret coiled around his neck and watched me with bright black eyes. The ferret wore a gold collar studded with red stones. Greg caressed him with one hand and nodded calmly to me, as if seeing me didn't surprise him.

I recognized some of the people—the man from the convenience store who also sold small carvings of animals and the nurse from my doctor's office, the one who always asked me about my artwork and once showed me the bracelet she'd made of small green shells.

I saw three other girls, perhaps a little older than I, carrying cats, and a boy who was younger, who came with a brown Great Dane.

They all held colored stones in their hands, clear stones about the size and shape of small eggs, and I was sure something moved inside those stones, something winged, captured but free.

Everyone sat on the ground in a circle.

I sat between Cait and the boy with the Great Dane.

"She has joined us," Cait said, smiling.

Everyone murmured and nodded.

Cait took a pink stone from the pocket of her tunic. It was transparent, and in its heart I saw something, like the petal of a rose. It moved as if a light wind stirred it. I was transfixed by it.

Cait held it out to me and I took it. It was warm and smooth, and when I held it closer to my face, the petal inside trembled.

I looked closer. The petal unfolded and I saw a world in it, a whole singing world, a true world, not a dreaming one, a world with no nightmares, no lonely people, no one who was sick or lost or afraid.

I saw that the others had put their stones on the ground in front of them, so I put mine there, too. A golden light suddenly sprang to life and linked the stones. The circle of the Other Ones had formed. The familiars leaned against their people, occasionally nuzzling them for attention.

"We've waited for you," Miss Ireland said.

"We knew you'd come," two girls said in unison, and both leaned forward to smile at me.

"You don't have to be afraid here," the nurse said.

"We'll answer all your questions," Mr. Oliver said. His familiar yawned and several of the Others laughed softly.

All of them looked at me expectantly then. If I'd had any questions, I'd forgotten them.

"I wondered if everything at school would get even worse," the boy with the Great Dane said.

"Did it?" I asked, afraid of the answer.

He shook his head and rubbed the dog's ears. "It got better. And I got better."

"I don't understand."

"I stayed out of all their dreams," he said quietly. "You'll see."

"Each dawn opens a new door to what is good," said the man who carved animals.

"Each twilight leads us to a peaceful rest," someone else said.

"We wondered if we'd ever have friends," said one of the girls.

"We have us," added the other.

I leaned forward and a light from my stone flared delicately. "Xiii said I am the threshold," I said. "What did he mean?"

"From the beginning," a tall young woman said, "each of us has been a threshold. Gifts pass through us. Healing, compassion, and safety flow into the world. We create. We build."

They released me from all my fears. I asked more questions then, and they answered.

When we were done at last, taking time that felt like no time at all, Cait asked me, "Wicce, what is your name?"

"I am Bridget!" I said. And I knew then that being Bridget was better than anything I had ever hoped for.

When it was over, I walked back to my house alone, holding the stone in one hand pressed to my chest. I wasn't afraid. My powers, let loose from my efforts to push them down, now flooded me. I was stronger than I had been. I was whole.

I didn't feel the cold until I reached my bedroom. Quickly, I hung the robe back in the closet and put on warm clothes and shoes. I tucked the stone in the pocket of my jeans. Bingo, stretched out on my bed, watched me leave.

The rain began again, pouring down harder than ever. I held up my hand and the rain parted over me in an arch as I crossed the street. I didn't knock on Jordan's door but touched the stone to it and when it opened, I entered quietly.

I heard Jordan coughing in the living room. I raised my hand and the rooms were lighted by the same light that had illuminated the forest where I accepted my craft that night.

Jordan lay on the couch, wrapped in blankets. He didn't see me. His eyes were half closed, his breathing labored.

"Jordan," I said.

His body didn't move but his mind fixed on me.

"It's time to go," I said.

We left and climbed the hill to Althea's house where I knew that she and her family huddled together in a corner of the dusty dark. The ground beneath my feet was soaked with rain. I felt it stir. I heard the growl of the earth beginning to slip toward the edge of the cliff.

I touched Althea's door with my stone and the door opened. "Althea, it's time to leave this place," I called out.

She and her parents appeared out of the dark, subdued by grief, unable to help themselves, unable even to change back to their true forms.

"We're trapped here," Althea said. "We can't leave."

"Come outside, into the light," I said.

"But it's dark," Althea's father said. "Too dark for us to fly."

"It's light," I said. "Come out."

I led them out of the house. The light, flickering pearl and gold, surrounded us, but beneath us I felt the earth trembling.

Althea and her parents looked up into the light, and after a moment, they dimmed and then faded. Then three falcons struggled free and flew up.

"What is the fee for our freedom, wicce?" called Althea's father.

"No fee," I said. I put my hand on Jordan's shoulder. "I ask a favor. Take him with you as far as the wind's gate and then let him go."

The falcons dropped to the edge of the roof. "We have never done that," Mr. Peale said.

"But you can," I said.

"Is it his time?" Mrs. Peale asked.

"His time is nearly here, but the last days are too hard. Let him fly."

Althea said, "She helped me, Father. Let him fly."

Jordan looked at me, barely aware. Even in spirit, he was weak and ill. "Should I go?"

"They know the way out of the dream," I said.

I waited while he looked up, first at the falcons and then higher, at distant stars that glittered through the pale pearl light. Mikey ran joyously between constellations.

Jordan smiled.

I held the stone between my hands and looked into it until I saw the dream end. When I looked up, four falcons flew up through the light. The wind from the stars caught them and they circled higher. Then the wind parted, and I saw the clear dark and the stars and the world at the end of all dreams.

One falcon soared through the gate.

The other three turned and flew east, the light expanding ahead of them, lighting the way to the mountains.

The earth beneath me groaned.

I whirled and ran down the hill. Behind me, the cliff slid roaring into the Sound, taking with it the house and the trees.

Cait waited at my gate, rain falling around her. I was exhausted, too tired to protect myself from the storm.

Cait put her arms around me and sheltered me. "You'll be all right," she said. "But you could have chosen a simpler way to let him go."

I shook my head. "I wanted to see him with Mikey. No one else loved him."

"You did."

"I thought he was beautiful, and I was sorry for him. But we can't love just one person. We have to love them all."

Cait kissed my forehead and sent me in the house. I crawled into bed and slept without dreaming.

But in my sleep, I heard sirens in the distance. The landslide had been discovered. I slept on.

Friday morning I made my way down the road that was finally drying after all the rain. Dad had asked me to work in the store helping Greg clear away the storm damage.

In the woods, the leaves left on the trees were gold and

red, like a treasure displayed just for me. I passed Jordan's house without looking at it. Eventually someone would notice that it had been abandoned.

On my way to the store, I looked up at the bright, windless sky and thought about the spring that would follow winter. Another school year would end. I saw my future, the house by the creek, and the white horse I'd ride. What happened in the dreams of others wouldn't matter. I was content in the present, with the stone in my pocket and all my questions answered, even the ones I hadn't known I'd ask.

When I reached the store, I found Greg sweeping leaves off the front walk. He looked up and asked, "What are you grinning about?"

"I was thinking about a white horse," I said.

He looked back down again and smiled.

I got a broom from the storeroom and worked beside him in companionable silence for several minutes.

"How's Jordan getting along?" he asked finally. "Have you talked to him lately?"

"He left to stay with friends," I said.

"Oh, good," he said.

He wouldn't know for certain that I'd helped Jordan, not unless I wanted him to know. And I didn't. When we help, we must never tell.

"The new girl moved away, too," I added. "Her family hated it here."

"Is that so?" Greg asked. He didn't seem especially interested.

I concentrated on my work. I'd nearly swept two tree spirits off the walk with the leaves. They chirped in annoyance and fluttered away to sit on a bare branch hugging each other. Greg saw them and grinned.

Dad came out and took Greg away to help him fix the broken panes in the greenhouse. I stopped and looked up at the broad arch of brilliant sky.

Nearby, a cat cried out, sounding cranky. I looked over my shoulder and saw a fat yellow tabby picking her way disgustedly across the muddy street.

"Xiii says hello," the cat said crossly. "He's impossible, you know. He could have sent me to the house, but no, he sends me here and now I suppose I'll have to hang around until you finally go home and we'll *walk* the whole way."

I almost smiled, but I knew better. This was a crucial moment, even if this being who would be my companion for life was as grouchy as my threshold guardian had been. "You're a friend of his?" I asked.

The cat sighed. "Not really. Who could want to be his friend? He picks his teeth with . . . things."

"What's your name?" I asked.

She lifted one paw and touched it to the ground. Three symbols appeared there, glimmered for a moment, and then vanished.

"What did they say?" I asked.

The cat sighed again. "That is my name. Nimuë." She looked at me sharply. "*Nim*-oo-aye. At least, that's what I've called myself for sixteen hundred of your years. Who can say what I'll call myself next time."

"Nimuë," I said, pleased with the sound of it.

"Yes," she agreed. "It *is* nice. Now let's talk about that dog. He can't eat from my dish, you know. And there are other things—"

"Don't worry," I said hastily. "I'll take care of everything."

"I *never* worry," Nimuë said. She found a spot in the sun that satisfied her and curled up for a nap.

I still had several feet of sidewalk to sweep before I could leave, so I went back to work. And then I realized what a picture we made.

A witch and her cat and her broom.

Somewhere, far away, I heard xiii laughing.

Jean Thesman has written several award-winning novels for young adults. She lives in Washington State.